I0713980

"Time and the Bear" originally printed in *Cry Baby Bridge* (Speculation Publications, 2023).

First edition independently printed 2023.
This edition printed 2024 by Pope Lick Press.

DEREK HEATH

MOONDISC

WITH BONUS STORY:

TIME AND THE BEAR

POPE LICK PRESS

2024

CONTENTS

PART ONE

HUNTER GATHERING

1:

ARRIVAL

Hooves crunched on a thick bed of gravel chips as the cab slipped through the wrought iron gates. The gates were glorious and obnoxiously decadent, tall banks of thick black spikes opening like wings in the moonlight. The evening air smelled of pine and rich, ripe earth.

With a tug of the reins, the carriage pulled to a stop. Slowly, a pale shape leaned out, passing a small tip to the guard who'd let them in. As the guard gratefully took the note, his partner winched the gates closed again. There was a loud squeal.

"Say," came the gruff voice of the pale thing as it slid back into the cab. It nodded toward the gates. "Will those things be enough to keep everything in?"

"Oh, I should think so, sir," the guard smiled thinly, the thick tufts of a glorious black moustache glittering with evening dew on his upper lip. "Nothing's escaped just yet."

"Good stuff," said the man in the carriage, his voice the thick timbre of somebody smoking a cigar while rolling his own loose teeth about in his throat, his own beard a shining moonlit grey. Oswald turned to smile at his travelling companions, his pale face lambent with excitement. "I should hate for my prey to get away from me so easily."

"Quite, father," murmured the young woman sitting across from him, rolling her eyes and turning to look into the trees. "Heaven forbid."

The estate was enormous, the expansive gardens filtering into a thick forest of pine and aspen that sprawled across the tall, brickwork walls. Henrietta hadn't yet seen the house itself, but she had a feeling its shadow had already fallen across the cab's roof. Across from her, the girl's mother clutched Oswald's hand and smiled excitedly. An assortment of bags lay around them, and a pair of large weapons cases had been set carefully on the seat next to Henrietta. She sat quite deliberately at an angle that did little to separate her from them – indeed, they were large enough that she hardly had room to sit – but quite effectively highlighted her distaste.

"Onward!" called her father, rapping on the cab's ceiling. A sharp snap of the reins and the vehicle was moving again, rattling over the driveway. Behind them, the guard was already returning to his post by the gates, hands stuffed into the thick leather belt of a regal purple uniform. Oswald beamed at his daughter, then laid a hand on his wife's knee and turned to her. "I'm so thrilled for you ladies to meet our host. You know, I've only met him the once, but I've heard stories of this man that you would not believe. What adventures! What a life!"

The cab rumbled on, leaving the gates behind and swaying as it bent around the winding driveway. On either side of the track to the estate, vast planes of grass became wild and loud with life, the red trunks of trees exploding up at the edges of the forest where the shadows became enormous and looming.

Amber lights streamed like greasy flares through the manor house's windows, orange fire blazing in the horses' eyes as the carriage pulled to a stop beside a pair of motorcars, their headlamps just as furiously ignited. The cab was finally still.

From somewhere in the woods came the long, low rumble of something large and hungry.

The front door swung open silently on well-oiled hinges, an arced wedge of lamplight collapsing onto the great stone steps and illuminating the trio standing upon them. A young dark-haired girl stepped into the light with a smile, her outfit immediately evincing her position as the maid of the house. She was denuded, however, of the posture of a professional housekeeper, and looked too young to have earned the role of greeter – officially, at least. Looking her over carefully, Oswald's daughter deduced that she was around her age.

"Good evening," the girl in the maid's outfit supplied, her voice a chipped mix of English and American accents. "The Heller party, I presume?"

"Quite right," said the oldest of the three. Oswald was a stout man with pudgy red cheeks and a spattering of blackheads in the rings around his eyes. He removed his bowler to reveal a combover of thin, shock-white hair, his scalp shiny with sweat beneath. He introduced himself curtly, then turned to gesture toward his companions. "Oswald. My wife, Alicia, and my daughter. Henrietta. We're here for the… weekend's event."

"Henry," his daughter offered, smiling thinly. "I prefer. Rather than Henrietta."

The girl in the doorway nodded politely, glancing in Henry's direction and allowing her gaze to linger for just half a second too long. Oswald's daughter had acquired her mother's looks: she was tall, with thick sandy hair cut to shoulder-length and pinned behind her head in a mess of loose curls. Her eyes sparkled a sharp blue, like ice, in the moonlight.

The maid smiled, offering a smile to both of Henrietta's parents before gesturing them inside. "Please do come and make yourselves comfortable.

The others are here, so I'm sure you'll be pleased to know the party has already begun."

"Oh, quite pleased," the portly bearded man said, returning his bowler to his head and glancing behind them. "You'll bring our bags up to our quarters, won't you, Lionel?"

A hunched figure with long, greasy black hair was already busying himself with removing those bags from the cab. "Aye, sir," he said, tossing them a throwaway smile before heaving a rifle case onto his shoulder. "I'll have 'em up in no time, so I will."

"Excellent stuff." Oswald Heller turned back to the maid, rubbing his stubby hands together. "Show us to the party."

2:

THE COLLECTIVE NOUN FOR 'HUNTER'

The manor house was enormous, a labyrinth of gilded stairwells and pearl-white ceilings through which shadows seemed to waft like ghostly creatures. The entrance hall was larger than the Hellers' apartment, though Henry had a feeling her father wouldn't be admitting that information aloud anytime soon. They were encouraged to keep their shoes on, and Oswald's Cuban heels clapped loudly on the tiles as they moved. Henry found herself gazing up into the ceiling, miles above them, the dizzying spiral of an enormous walnut staircase ploughing into the far reaches of the pearly room. The walls were filled with portraits in gilded frames, and many of them seemed to watch her. Clattering explosions of noise came from the kitchens and, even as they were led to the drawing room, the Hellers had to pause to allow a small train of waiters through with sparkling silver dishes of canapes and drinks.

The bustling hive of the drawing room parted for them as they entered, a dozen or so strangers casting wide, white grins in their direction. Henry swallowed as she followed her parents through the moulded plasterwork of the doorframe, feeling quite underdressed in her coat and skirt. She hung back with the maid as Oswald and Alicia Heller melted into the crowd with a warble of greetings. Her father was doing that awful handshake of his where he seemed to clap somebody's entire forearm in both of his and shake their whole body. Henry swallowed nervously, looking about the room as a sea of faces swam in her vision.

"You don't come to many of these, do you?" the maid whispered beside her.

Henry glanced in the girl's direction and smiled weakly. "Not really my sort of thing. Father insisted. He usually does. My mother"—she glanced into the throng of the party, where Alicia Heller was giggling at some joke made by a broad-shouldered Black woman with filo crumbs on her dress—"threatened to pull me out of school if I didn't humour them just once."

"I can summarise the room for you, if you'd like." Another whisper, almost too low to hear, and Henry found herself moving almost subconsciously closer to the maid. Only to hear her better, she convinced herself quickly, and not because she smelled pleasant and warm.

"Henry smiled. "That would be helpful.""

"Well, they're all arseholes."

Henry's mouth opened, her eyebrows cocking a little at the absurd bluntness of the remark. "You can't say that!" she giggled. "I thought you meant—"

"I did, I did," the maid said quietly, pulling Henry to one side as another waitress bustled past them. "All right, let me run you through everyone here. Properly, this time."

"Properly? Are you sure?" Henry said.

"I promise," the maid grinned. "So, the couple your parents are talking to right now are Cavan and Mary Gilmour. They come to every event. He works in oil, though I'm not sure 'work' is the correct term for buying a big pump and sending good people down into the crust of the Earth. I believe Mary's a painter. Also oils, funnily enough."

"Arseholes?"

"Most definitely," the maid smiled wickedly, moving on quickly with a brief, if less-than-subtle, point into the corner of the drawing room. Beside a tall, loudly-snicking grandfather clock, a pair of gentlemen in regal cream suits – buttoned smartly, almost like military uniforms – seemed to be silently surveying the room. The taller of the two pinched a flute of champagne in one hand, while his partner – standing around five-foot-four, if one subtracted the height of his hairpiece – chewed a gritty-looking cigar. "*Those* arseholes are Ronald and Louis Harcourt. French. If you spend more than thirty seconds with either of them, they'll tell you about the time they wrestled a rhino into the ground with their bare hands and blew off its horn with a stick of dynamite."

"Ugh," Henry muttered. "And her? The woman by the window?"

The two of them looked across the drawing room where, behind Henry's parents and the Gilmours, a tall, pretty older woman with thick grey hair and a flocked red petticoat looked out toward the woods at the edge of the estate's colossal grounds. She seemed oblivious to the conversations bubbling around her and evidently hadn't indulged in any of the hors d'oeuvres, for her white-gloved hands were pristine. Her dark skin was dappled by the moonlight filtering through the shallow distortions in the glass. Her eyes were bright and carefully observant.

"I don't know," the girl confessed hesitantly. "I've never seen her at one of these before."

"And what about you?" Henry said, turning to her. "I never asked your name."

"Oh," the girl said, flushing a little. A strand of dark, almost-black hair had fallen in her eye and she shivered it away. "Darcy. I work for Mr. Roman. Speaking of which, I should probably get back to it. You'll be all right?"

"If you come back," Henry smiled.

Darcy's lips parted, but she said nothing.

"Sorry, I… yes. I will," Darcy said, "I'll be fine, thank you."

The maid smiled brightly back at her before slinking back into the entrance hall.

Henry turned back to the room. The party was smaller than she had imagined: Ronald and Louis Harcourt seemed to occupy half of a room, although they were quite narrow and not exactly moving much. The other half was filled with the leering conversation of her parents and the Gilmours. The Black woman by the window took up hardly any room at all, but the mystery surrounding her seemed to drift into everything; their host had picked a rather small room, in fact, to hole them away in, and Henry couldn't help but wonder if that was deliberate. The party seemed so much bigger in the drawing room than they would have out in the entrance hall. Induced claustrophobia. Very effective.

Henry grimaced as she noted her parents beckoning her over, no doubt desperate to introduce her to some of the others. She shuddered and glanced about, finally noticing that Roman himself, the owner of the manor and host of the 'event' for which everybody had attended, was not present. At least, Darcy hadn't pointed him out, and if he were about she imagined most of the preening nobs in the drawing room would be fawning over him.

"Ah, fuck this," she muttered, ignoring her parents' gestures and stepping back into the hallway. She raised her hand to signal a nearby butler and when he started over she said, a little sheepishly, "I'm so sorry, where's the bathroom?"

3:

THE THING ON THE MANTELPIECE

"You know, I heard he entertained Spencer Barron – the author?" Cavan was saying, his ruddy cheeks glistening as he swilled a glass of red wine beneath his nose. "I suppose he's had all manner of celebrities in this very room."

"Barron?" Oswald Heller said, wrinkling his nose a little. "Never heard of the chap. What does he write, poetry?"

"Oh, no – *horror*," Cavan said, both of his eyebrows furrowing into a mysteriously sweaty knot. "I believe he was one of those sort of Gothic types, churning out ghastly ghost stories here and there and turning a profit off of… well, *disturbing* people."

"I believe the younger generation are quite hooked on the stuff nowadays," Cavan's wife nodded. Mary turned to the Hellers: "What about your daughter, does she enjoy the bloodier stuff?"

"Our daughter?" Oswald frowned. Momentarily he looked bewildered. Then the look seemed to pass from his face, as if he'd temporarily forgotten her altogether. "Oh, of course. No, no, Henry isn't into all that. Not at all. I must say, I'm not sure *what* her interests tend to at the moment… funny creatures, aren't they?"

"Daughters?" Cavan said.

"Women," Oswald smirked, and the two of them laughed smugly.

"Remarkable," Alicia said, hooking her arm around her husband's and shooting a bemused look in Mary Gilmour's direction. "I must say, I think I *have* heard of this Barron fella – wasn't there some scandal last year when the poor fellow wound up in the river?"

"Killed himself," Cavan nodded grimly. "Though they do say his *body* was never found, only his personal effects – his wife was quite distraught, I imagine."

"I dare say," Mary rolled her eyes. She huffed, glancing toward the grandfather clock. "You know, I understand being fashionably late, but for our host to leave us waiting *quite* so long—"

"Probably busying himself with one of his experiments," Oswald murmured, "I believe he's quite the scientist… a somewhat 'experimental' hobbyist, if you understand me."

"A scientist? Good lord, what *isn't* the man?!" Cavan said. "Explorer, adventurer, archaeologist – I wonder quite how he finds the time to sleep!"

Beside the window, the tall Black woman with the red flocked dress turned her head a little, her ears discretely pricked up.

Henry had managed to locate the bathroom perfectly well, but returning through the labyrinth to the drawing room proved disproportionately challenging.

She must have been somewhere on the ground floor still, for she had not encountered any staircases, though she felt as if she were in a different building altogether: she recognised few of the narrow corridors she had wound her way through in the past few minutes. Despairingly, she called out: "Darcy? Mr. Roman? Is anybody here?"

She turned a corner and exhaled, relieved, at the sight of a grand oak door at the end of the corridor. It seemed obnoxious enough to lead through to the hallway, she thought, picking up her skirts and advancing with some haste.

"Thank goodness," she said as she wrenched the knob and pulled the door open, more for her own benefit really than that of any waiting staff or guests loitering on the other side. Hurriedly she stepped through. "I thought myself quite—"

She stopped, her breath hitching in her throat.

Henry's eyes flitted left and right in a fruitless attempt to take in the enormous room splayed out before her.

"…lost."

The ceiling was ridiculously high and all the walls were stacked with shelves and wooden racks. The tiled floor was piled with heaps of linen-covered boxes and baskets; round, wooden tables were scattered about and covered in yet more of the things. A grand fireplace seethed quietly to her left, the dying embers of a fire smouldering in its mouth.

Before she could stop herself Henry had stepped into the room, gazing in awe at the collection of unknowable things gathered in here. The walls were plain and the wide, grand windows opposite the fireplace were covered with plush purple curtains. Everything was polished, neatly arranged – save for the scattered things on the tables which evidently hadn't yet found their place – and it was apparent that the owner of all these strange things spent quite an amount of time in the room with them. The smell of dry wood and hearthsmoke followed her around the room.

"Wow," Henry whispered as she moved to the nearest wall, admiring a vast assortment of Aztec spears and tall, brightly-painted wooden shields all neatly bracketed to the plasterboard. Farther along the wall was a row of gaping masks, their eyes and mouths outlined in stark white against the flaring blues, reds and greens of painted colours she'd never seen before.

Turning, she saw more on the opposite wall, along with a bookshelf stacked with all sorts of mechanical equipment: strange clockwork devices ticked quietly between displays of elegantly-carved ivory artworks and black, charcoal bones decorated with gold inlay. An enormous glass cylinder stood in one corner, green fluid bubbling excitedly inside; behind the door through which she'd entered, various animal skins hung on hooks, shimmering colourfully in the faded firelight and the glow of a series of electrical lamps on the walls. There was something beautiful about those coats, despite the grim nature of their origin. As she spun she noted deer skulls pinned to the walls, dozens of them, and other trophies which were decidedly less familiar. The bone-white face of a great eyeless beast stared at her from beside one window, its teeth firmly locked in a deathly grimace; it might have been a bear's, though it was surely far too large.

Henry turned back to the fireplace, raising her fingers to run them along the ledge of a smooth, marble mantelpiece. Photographs of a slender Black man in khaki hunting gear were displayed proudly in stately frames: one where he was standing over the carcass of a deflated, raggedy-maned lion; another where he held a bundled antelope corpse in each hand, their heads dragging on the ground. A white-hot bolt of rage shot through Henry's chest as she moved to the centre of the mantelpiece, where a large bell jar stood between two more photographs.

She stopped here, watching the thing inside the bell jar as though expecting it to move.

The object sat on a small black plinth inside the jar, suspended in the air so that, through the curved glass – which also distorted its size somewhat – it appeared to be floating six inches off the mantel. It was about the size of her palm, and almost flat: a slight, shallow bowl of white stone, inverted so that it was rendered as a dome, rather than a crater. A convex disc of ivory.

Gently, hypnotised by the thing, Henry moved her hand forward to lift the glass and get a better look.

"Quite remarkable, isn't it?" came a soft voice from behind her.

Henry's blood ran cold and she swiftly withdrew her hand, turning her head to look in the direction of the doorway.

The tall Black man from the photographs stood there, hands behind his back, dressed not in his hunting gear but a smart blue tuxedo, his lapels flocked and the cummerbund around his narrow waist a pleasant shining shade of aqua. He smiled kindly, his eyes dark and glinting in the light.

"I'm sorry, I wasn't—"

"No," he said gently, raising a hand. "No, don't apologise."

Stepping forward, he lowered his hand again and nodded toward the thing in the bell jar.

"Do you like it?"

"What is it?" Henry said.

"I call it the *Moondisc*," the tall man smiled. Standing closer to her now, Henry noticed that he had brought a new smell into the room: the ripe, not-unpleasant scent of stewing meat. "Quite small, quite insignificant among my other… artefacts… but stirring, nonetheless."

"Mr. Roman," Henry realised.

"Wayne," the man insisted, offering his hand. She shook it hesitantly and he nodded back toward the door. "I assume your parents are this way?"

"I hope so – I'm sorry, I didn't mean to pry, I—"

"Oh, no. Not at all." He grinned. "Even I get lost sometimes. Shall we?"

Henry nodded thankfully and the tall man slipped his arm into the crook of her elbow, gently guiding her back to the door.

Behind them, the Moondisc hung quietly in its jar, absolutely still and speckled – though the marks were difficult to discern through the glass – with a collection of tiny pockmarks and pores and jagged, lighting-bolt ridges.

"Why is it called that?" Henry said, glancing back toward the thing one last time. "Is it… is it made of moon? Did it fall to the Earth?"

"You could say that," Roman smiled, and he led her out into the corridor.

4:

AN EXPERIMENT IN MEAT

"Thank you all for waiting so patiently," Roman called, silencing the room as he stepped in – so tall, Henry noted, that he towered a good six inches above anybody else in there – and spreading his hands warmly. "My dear guests, friends – returning and new – I must apologise for my tardiness. I have promised you all an event like none that you have attended before, and I must confess, preparations for such a thing have kept me away from many of my duties. But I am thrilled to confirm that everything is finally ready!"

At this there was slight murmuration of triumphant mutters, and Henry took the opportunity to slither into the drawing room and join her parents by a lush, cushioned chaise longue. "Where on earth have you been?" her mother chided out of the corner of her mouth.

"Peeing," Henry hissed back.

"Now, as usual," Roman continued, striding confidently toward the nearest guests and taking their hands one at a time, "I have selected for you a collection of exotic animals – good evening, Ronnie – and nice to see you again, Lou – and they have made themselves quite at home on the grounds. Now, the rules are the same as always; for the fee you have paid, you are welcome to explore the grounds as you wish – though I would ask that you refrain from entering the icehouse; any changes in temperature can have quite a dramatic effect in there, as I'm sure you can imagine – and any kill that you secure is yours to do with as you wish. Welcome, Mr. Gilmour. Mrs. Gilmour, resplendent as ever.

"Now," he straightened up, one hand clamped firmly inside Oswald Heller's while the other gestured all around, "While I have invited you to the estate before to hunt boar, wild cats, even rhinoceros, I would like to promise you right here – right now – that the beasts I have managed to procure for your hunting pleasure *this* year are… well…"

He leaned in, grinning devilishly inches from Oswald's face.

"*Spectacular*," he whispered. "Good to see you, old chap."

"When does the hunt begin?" Ronnie Harcourt

called, his brother nodding beside him.

"Tomorrow morning at dawn," Roman supplied loudly, briefly clasping Alicia Heller's hand in his own. He winked down at Henry and turned back to the room. "However, so that we may begin the celebrations a little early… how about a friendly contest, tonight, to determine who among you might gain a small headstart?"

There was a faint rumble among them.

"Follow me to the ballroom," Roman grinned. "I think you're going to like this."

The ballroom was on the second floor, and indeed seemed to take up half of it. They climbed slowly, bundling each other excitedly up the colossal stairs until they reached what was, perhaps, the largest room Henry had ever found herself in. The ballroom was a titanic spectacle of arched plasterwork and tall, narrow windows, gas lamps flaring along one wall and bleeding onto the windowpanes as warped blobs of amber. It was longer than it was wide, and the floor was hard polished pine.

Wayne Roman had laid out what looked like a small shooting range in the room, with a crude firing bay near the door: a selection of round wooden tables, covered with cloth, arranged in a line that crossed the width of the room. Upon each table was a pistol, a long-barrelled, ugly hunk of a thing that seemed to smoulder gently beside a tin of round lead balls.

Roman grinned as the guests looked confusedly at each other. Slipping between two of the tables, he marched into the centre of the empty ballroom and gestured vaguely. "Please, direct yourselves to a table each," he said. "I shall explain the rules."

Hesitantly, most of the guests filtered toward the tables, each selecting an identical pistol and watching the tall man with a mixture of bemused entertainment and dismay.

Henry looked across at the older Black lady in the red velvet dress. She looked back, seemingly just as reluctant to step up to any of the tables.

There came the sound of something dragging over the wood, and Henry turned her attention back to the ballroom, stepping forward to get a better look at what Roman was doing. Her father had elbowed his way to the table in the middle of the row, and beside him Lou Harcourt was stubbing out his cigar on the tablecloth. At the far end of the room Cavan and Mary Gilmour had chosen two tables next to each other.

"That's it, that's it, everybody step up," Roman said gleefully, his words somehow seeming to be directed right at her. Was she a part of this? She knew she'd rather not be, but it didn't seem she had much choice. Reluctantly she stepped up to an empty table between her mother and Ronnie Harcourt, eyeing the pistol with distaste. Elsewhere, the tall older woman seemed to have done the same.

She looked up and saw that their host had dragged a large, box-shaped thing into the centre of the ballroom. Though it was covered with a thick cloth it was evidently some item of furniture, something shaped like a small wardrobe on poorly-oiled wheels. Clapping his hands together as he straightened up, Roman continued:

"Now, most of you shall begin your hunt tomorrow at dawn," he said, "but to add a little fire to the competition, I thought I'd offer one of you – that's *one* of you, not one party – the chance to step out into the grounds a few minutes early."

There were some vague murmurs; most seemed annoyed at the possibility of being second onto the field, while all of the complaints were tinged with a shred of optimism as the protestors seemed to realise that they might, if successful, be able to see everybody *else* take second. The idea of a head-start seemed particularly appealing to Henry's father, who had never been an extraordinarily successful hunter. She watched him flexing his fingers as Roman spoke, itching to get his hands on the gun no matter what the challenge offered might be.

Then she heard something.

A gentle thumping: the sound of something moving beneath the cover.

"Many of you have attended events here and been entertained with displays of groundbreaking science," Roman continued, speaking more seriously now. Shoving his hands into his pockets, he said, "As you might know, I have spent most of my life travelling the world, dabbling in the practices of other cultures... other worlds. Collecting resources, tampering with the dazzling fabric of reality itself. I regret to inform you that my laboratory is still off-limits during your stay here, but I am delighted to present to you a compromise: an experiment. A product of my scientific dabblings. Seen by no eyes but your own... *behold*!"

With that he turned and whipped back the cover with a flourish and the *snap* of thick linen on the wooden floor. The thing beneath the cover was revealed: not a wardrobe but a cage, about the size of a dresser with hay sparsely scattered across its earthen floor, thick iron bars half-obscuring the thing inside. It was awful.

Somewhere in the ballroom, somebody screamed; Henry thought it might have been Mrs. Gilmour, though she couldn't be sure the shriek wasn't her own.

Roman grinned wickedly. "Whoever kills it gets an early start," he said, and he reached out to throw across a thin, brass bolt and open the cage.

There was a moment of bewildered near-silence as the creature was released from its cage, then at once somebody across the room yelled gruffly, "Gracious me, what the devil is that?"

Henrietta Heller just stared as the rest of them started to scream, scrabbling madly for their pistols. A pungent mixture of shock and excitement filled the cloying air between them and the first shot went off before she had time to register what she was seeing; the smacking report of the pistol echoed in her ears and lead punched into the ballroom wall, splintering the plaster. Roman had disappeared, leaping to safety somewhere to the side of the room.

The creature crawled wetly out of the cage, a mess of spidery legs and bulging tissue. It moved quickly, insect-like despite the thick, muscular sacs of red-raw meat that made up its segmented abdomen. Scuttling around the back of the cage, it quickly reared up and loomed over the bars, stretching its body so that it was as tall as any of them.

Its face was distinctly human, and the stitches were plainly visible where the edges had been fused to the cranium of some other poor creature. Its eyes flitted from side to side as its mouth opened, lips separating to reveal a pair of pincered mandibles clicking hungrily together. The skin of the face was pale – dead – and the striations up and down its body were an awful oily blue.

Another shot rang out and the creature's head whipped around. It hissed in the direction of the shooter – one of the Harcourt brothers, Henry thought vaguely – and slithered over the cage, leaving trails of red-yellow fluid where its body dragged along the bars. Bolts and industrial-looking staples pinned each clawed, multiple-jointed leg to its body, rivers of poorly-stitched meat running across it like stripes. It was a haphazard abomination, parts taken from dead things and sewn together; it was like nothing she had ever seen.

The loud *clap* of another pistol, right by her ear, restarted her fluttering heart and Henry dry-heaved, cringing as more bullets flew. The excitement was palpable and it translated to a hazy crossfire of wild misses and ricochets, tearing the ballroom apart. Something clipped one of the creature's awful legs and ripped a great chunk of chitinous flesh loose; it wheeled around and its eyes locked on Henry's.

Beside her, Ronnie Harcourt's smouldering pistol swung downward as he reloaded. The creature was partially blind; one of its eyes was rolling madly. It started toward her, scuttling over the floorboards, oblivious to the ribbons of meat that each graze and near-miss ripped from its back. Blood sprayed the walls as it skittered, grinning, a shining pincer opening up in its throat.

"What the…" Henry whispered, but there was no

question she could ask that would offer any kind of satisfying answer. She balked as the thing lurched forward, its one good eye locked on her, its body writhing as it moved closer, closer, evidently having picked her out as the one thing in the room not trying to kill it, as a target, then it was leering above her, its throat clicking loudly, one eye rolling and insane while the other was mad with bloodlust—

Before she could stop herself Henry had jammed a ball into the gun and fired, squeezing the trigger with two fingers. Her wrist shuddered as the pistol kicked back, its report joining dozens of others and echoing about the room.

The creature's head caved in and a thick spray of red mist was sucked violently into the hole the bullet had made. It ripped out again through the abomination's neck and Henry dropped the gun, sinking back behind the others as the creature flopped to the floor, convulsing.

Henry stood, panting, incredulous. All the yelling and shooting had stopped; the ballroom was awfully silent.

"I wasn't… I didn't… it was going to…"

"We have a winner," Roman whispered, suddenly behind her, and as the ballroom slowly erupted into a cacophony of tossed-away pistols and reluctant applause, she watched the thing's eyeballs swim in the ruined, wet cavern of its head and tried not to throw up.

PART TWO

THE
EXOTIC

5:

DAWN

Henry did not sleep easily that night.

Her father had largely ignored her over dinner, still frustrated that the prize had been rewarded to her instead of himself; meanwhile her mother was busy discussing the vast possibilities of science with Ronald and Louis Harcourt, who were significantly more talkative now that they had had a little to drink. Roman cleverly ignored many of the questions about his work, though he proudly admitted that the creation they had witnessed in the ballroom was just a part of the wondrous things he had planned. He completely blanked any questions about the kind of creatures they might have the pleasure of hunting in the forest the next day, though he assured an impatient Cavan Gilmour that they were to be far more exotic than anything he had encountered before.

That was the word he kept using. 'Exotic'.

Was that how he'd have described the thing upstairs, had it lived a little longer?

Henry's quarters were small but well-furnished, a four-poster bed filling most of the room. Her bags lay largely untouched, her nightclothes the only things she had retrieved from them so far. Her father's old hunting rifle had been tucked beneath the bed, where she'd hoped she might forget about it.

Strange sounds came from the woods as she tried to sleep.

At a little after midnight Henry slipped out of bed and moved to the window, listening closely. The whole estate seemed to rumble gently, to vibrate beneath her feet as though some colossal machinery were whirring underground; but there were other sounds, organic sounds from outside. Low chirrups and bellows, noises unlike any she'd heard before.

Heaving the window open, she looked into the trees and listened.

For a moment there was nothing, and then there came a faint cry, almost ape-like, followed by a low, quiet rumble.

There were things out there, parading the grounds, sticking to the trees where they could move unseen.

She would see them soon enough.

Climbing back into bed, she lay there awake for most of the night before finally succumbing to her exhaustion and falling into a hot, disturbed sleep.

Downstairs, the Moondisc sat still in its glass prison. The edges of the shallow, bowl-like dish were serrated, as if they had been chipped at with tiny teeth, or the edge of a saw.

Even in the dark, the white stony thing seemed to catch a faint kind of light from somewhere.

A little before dawn Henry found herself on the stone steps outside the front door, a small crowd of seething onlookers watching her from the entrance hall behind. She could feel her father's eyes drilling into the back of her head; worse, however, was the bony hand on her shoulder. She looked up.

"Ready?" said Wayne Roman, dressed now in a dark pinstriped suit and far too chipper for four in the morning. It was still dark outside, though she had noted a ring of floodlights around the edges of the estate, and wondered how much of the forest was infused with their glow. Not much, she supposed.

"Fine," she said, adjusting the rifle strapped to her back. It was heavy; her father had abandoned the Farquharson single-shot a few years ago for the Winchester 54, leaving the stalking rifle to his daughter. She hated it.

"Ladies and gentlemen," Roman declared proudly, swinging his whole body around to face everyone. As he spoke Henry peered into the trees, separated from the house only by that vast, neatly-clipped lawn. She saw nothing but shadow beneath the thick, full aspen trunks. Nothing but darkness. "We must all now return inside and regroup here in an hour's time, whence the hunt shall officially begin. For now, wish young Henrietta—"

"—Henry," she muttered, mostly to herself—

"—the best of luck!"

She stumbled forward as Roman nudged the small of her back.

"Remember," he whispered, "you're free to hunt anywhere in the grounds, just don't go into the icehouse."

She heard her mother call something out into the dark but before she could turn there was an almighty *slam* and the front door had closed.

Henry squeezed her eyes shut and swung the Farquharson off her back, checking it was loaded before gripping it firmly in both hands. She had switched her nightclothes for sensible hunting gear, and her belt was loaded with ammunition. She hoped not to have to use any of it. She had always been against hunting for sport, but growing up in the circles her parents had forced themselves into, she'd seldom been able to avoid it. She had a plan, though: she would find herself a spot on the edge of the woods and wait this out, returning to the house when she could see some of the others doing the same, likely dragging the carcasses of poor defiled creatures with them. Her own rifle, she had decided, was purely for protection.

There was no joy in this. No reward. She was disgusted by it, repulsed by it. And now she had no choice but to partake. Well, she would find some shelter and keep an eye out for signs that the end of the hunt was nigh; and, hey, if she happened to plant a bullet in one of the party members' legs – entirely by accident, of course; anything could happen – then so be it.

She crunched forward across the gravel.

"Psst!"

The sound came from somewhere to her left and she turned her head to look, spotting Darcy just a few yards away. The young maid stood with her back pressed to one of the estate building's many lime pillars, a network of ivy crawling up the wall behind her.

"I'm sorry," Darcy whispered as Henry approached her. "I heard what happened last night."

"What the hell was that thing?" Henry hissed.

Darcy shook her head. "My dad... he likes his experiments. I couldn't tell you anything about them. Only that I would be careful out there today."

"Your... dad? Wait, you know what's out there?"

"Adopted," she smiled weakly. "Listen, he plans on going down to the laboratory once the hunt begins proper. If you can find somewhere to camp out for an hour... maybe two... come back to the service door, all right? I'll let you in. I've got somewhere you can hide till all of this is done."

Henry hesitated. "You'd do that for me?"

Darcy seemed to flush again. "Couple hours," she said. "That's all."

"I'll see you then," Henry smiled. "Thank you. So much."

"Good luck."

Drawing in a deep breath, Henrietta Heller gripped her rifle tight and marched cautiously toward the woods.

Dawn split yolk-like across the horizon in a thin, seeping band of gold, chewing into the crust of all the broiling blue above the trees. A great horn signalled the beginning of the hunt; the guests formed their parties quickly and split across the grounds.

Oswald and Alicia Heller were joined by the Gilmours and the four of them headed tentatively into the woods, rifles cocked and ready. Mary Gilmour had claimed rather boldly earlier that morning that she preferred to use a handgun, but now that they had begun Oswald saw that she had opted for a Model 54 much like his own.

The treeline was a barrier between worlds; once they passed through it the darkness was enveloping and hungry, the silence overwhelming.

There was no birdsong, Alicia Heller noted uneasily.

Despite that, she felt as though they were being watched. The smell of pine was drowned out by a thick, sweaty film of anticipation that covered their little group. The trunks were close together, sparse clearings between them laid gently with blankets of dead leaves and bones; soon with the daylight the woods would look far different to this, but for now the light hardly entered through the thick, green canopy above and every trunk was the silhouette of a crooked arm jutting from the ground, every tree the tooth of some titanic maw that had swallowed them whole.

"We should find Henrietta," Alicia whispered to Mary Gilmour, the two of them moving forward while their husbands lingered back, swinging their rifles around to inspect every tree, every broken branch and heap of rotting deadfall. For a second, she found herself oddly confused: why was she so concerned about the girl? Then she remembered – of course, she was the girl's mother. She was *meant* to be concerned. Why had she forgotten that?

Why had she felt – just for a moment – like she had no responsibility for the girl at all?

"My poor darling is out here all alone…" she said, recovering herself quickly. She was tired, she thought, and stressed. That was all. She had just had a queer moment. "I wonder if we shouldn't abandon the hunt for now and dedicate ourselves to finding her."

"Oh, I'm sure she's quite all right," Mary said. "She seems fairly capable, if I may say so."

"Quiet!" hissed Cavan Gilmour behind them, raising one finger. "I hear something."

Oswald followed the man's gaze, raising his rifle into the trees over a small crest of dry earth. "Nothing there, my boy," he whispered.

Mary had lifted her rifle too and she peered in the direction they were looking. Nothing through the trees but an enormous oak which had fallen onto its side, a gargantuan nest of gnarled roots ripped out of the ground to form a small, moss-covered mountain of spikes and black needles.

"You're imagining things," Alicia hissed in Cavan's direction. "I'm going to go and find my—"

The dry, brittle snap of a dead branch behind the overturned oak. The great broken trunk of the thing shuddered as something moved behind it, shaking loose clumps of swampy black muck and thick clots of moss.

Alicia swallowed her words and lowered a hand to her own rifle, a polished Mauser '98, drawing back the bolt and sliding a bullet inside.

6:
THE SHIT

Ronald and Louis Harcourt had attended several of Roman's hunting events and largely knew the best spots for tracking; it seemed that whatever strange beasts the man imported and let loose on his grounds – around which, they had been assured, were walls inescapable to any creature they could imagine – they all gravitated to the same drinking locations, and tended to prefer the thick knots of pine at the very centre of the woods.

"Every time we visit I am reminded of the sheer size of the man's grounds," Lou murmured as they plunged deeper into the forest, heading in quite the opposite direction to the others. He had only recently begun chewing the cigar clamped between his teeth but already his chin was sprayed with earthy particles, the rich scent lifting into the air around them. "I only wonder how the bastard manages to maintain it all!"

"Probably helps that every one of us donated quite a large sum to be here," Ronnie said quietly, the 1886 Lebel steady in his hands. It was, he felt, far superior to his brother's Berthier, though he knew that at some point during the day they would switch weapons, as was their custom, to make slightly fairer the friendly competition between them.

"Suppose so," mumbled Lou. He paused. "D'you smell that, old chap?"

Sniffing, Ronald Harcourt shook his head. But he had seen something, and silently directed his brother's attention to it: a set of tracks on the ground, faint – a good few hours old and largely filled with dusty earth and mites of dead organic matter – and slipping into the trees before them.

"What is that, some kind of wild cat?" Lou hissed quietly. "*Mon Dieu*, the *paws* on that thing!"

"Let's find out," whispered Ronnie, nodding them forward.

Quietly they stalked through the trees, the pawprints more like scuffmarks; though they were clearly discernible in places, largely the tracks were vague scrapings in the dirt. A small, greenish pile of scat told them that the creature had passed between two aspen – one knocked down by lightning and leaning haphazardly in the branches of the other so that together they formed a sort of triangular archway – in the last hour.

They were just approaching the edge of a large clearing when Lou struck his brother in the chest with one hand, preventing him from going any further.

Ronnie was about to protest when he saw it.

"Oh, *nous sommes dans la merde*," Ronnie breathed, shaking his head and taking a cautious step back.

The thing in the clearing hadn't seen them yet, but he had no reason to doubt that its eyesight would be potent enough to catch them in a moment – however distracted it was. The creature was feasting, hunched over a carcass that was at first indistinguishable as anything more than a flayed hump of meat and muscle. As the brothers watched, it became clear that parts of that hump were non-organic in nature, and quickly Louis Harcourt recognised the uniform of one of Wayne Roman's waiters.

The man had been ripped apart, his chest and bowels open wide and spilling into the earth. One arm twitched as the creature dug its thick muzzle into the cavern of the poor man's chest, snuffling at his entrails.

The feeding animal was the size of a bear, but more dog-like in appearance; in truth, it was nothing at all like either. Its fur was oily black and it shivered over thick knots of muscle, the creature's back heaving as it slopped hunks of meat into its throat. Slivers of bone protruded from its shoulders like armour and thick, black spines quivered along its back, bunching into a needly mane around its neck.

"What the fuck is that?" Lou hissed.

Ronnie shook his head. "Back. Get back."

His heel tramped down a dry branch with a dull, hollow *snap*.

The creature froze.

"*Merde*," Ronnie echoed as it turned its great bear-like head to look in their direction, spiny knobs of bone forming a growling, pincered exoskeleton around its yawing mouth.

Three bright yellow eyes flared hungrily in its skull and it seemed to smile, ropes of blood hanging from its teeth.

Darcy stood beside the window in one of the estate's smaller kitchens, staring out into the sun.

Dawn was sliced open and the sky was a miasmic gold, pillows of cloud tinted yellow and screaming by the rising sun. Mist rolled about the treeline, slipping over gnarled roots and filtering through the wild grass at the edge of the wooded area. The grounds were over forty acres in total, the forested land making up around two-thirds of that; where most girls her age had memories of gardens and streets, hers were of isolation and silence.

She could hardly remember her life before Roman had adopted her. Didn't know her parents. Where she was from, even. There was no great mystery in it. She had come from somewhere else. And her parents… well, if they weren't dead, they might as well be.

She had asked Wayne Roman, once, why he had taken her in. And he had told her, in simple terms: he was lonely. For all his adventuring and hunting and travelling, all his experimentation and madness… he needed someone to share it all with. At the time, she had taken this as truth, but as she had grown older Darcy had realised that it wasn't *sharing* he was interested in. It was *impressing*.

He had adopted her so that he had someone to adore him.

Darcy watched anxiously as sunlight splayed itself across the treetops. Thick green needles rippled in a light wind; the branches creaked and groaned, though she couldn't hear them from here. Below her feet, something rumbled, the stone flags of the kitchen almost vibrating. Copper pans dangled from a rail behind her, swinging ever-so-softly as though caressed by ghostly fingers. The stove was alight, and a brass kettle had begun to whisper.

There was no sign of movement in the woods, though she doubted she would see anything from here. Still, she prayed that she might glimpse a flash of something – some sign that Henry was okay – a splash of colour, or a start of action…

There was something different about the girl. Darcy

had felt something in her stomach that was unfamiliar and terrifying when they had spoken, something knotted and cruel.

She *liked* her.

This was new. Darcy had only had very brief encounters with the outside world: she was home-schooled, and aside from Roman's guests, she hardly saw anybody at all. Sporadically she wandered into the village, but Roman had always made it very clear that she had everything she needed in the house, and there had only been scarce occasions she had been able to dispute that. He kept the larders well-stocked, and her room furnished with painting equipment and books, sometimes so efficiently that it seemed he was deliberately keeping her from leaving the manor.

"Come on…" she whispered to herself, leaning forward. She was gripping the sill with white knuckles, she realised, and she let go. Her stomach fluttered again. *Come on…*

"Spectating?" somebody said behind her.

Darcy almost yelped, jumping out of her skin as the voice startled her. Immediately her body was painted with gooseflesh and she turned, swallowing nervously. "Hmm?"

Roman leant against the doorframe, his arms folded across his chest. He smiled kindly, though it didn't reach his eyes. "The hunt," he said, nodding toward the window. "Perhaps you'd like to join in some day."

"Oh," Darcy smiled back weakly. "Perhaps."

She stepped away from the window, hurrying to the stove as the kettle's shrill whisper became a whistle.

"I was just having some tea. Would you like some?"

Roman shook his head. "That's all right, sweetheart, thank you."

He moved suddenly, straightening in the doorway before starting across the kitchen. Darcy watched the man out of the corner of her eye as she poured hot water, steam licking her fingers and threatening to scald them. Slowly Roman walked to the window, slipping his hands into his pockets. He had removed his suit jacket and his waistcoat was unbuttoned; his shirtsleeves were rolled up to the elbows.

He seemed to watch the woods for a moment. Darcy stirred, cringing at the plink of her teaspoon against the insides of the porcelain mug.

"What a beautiful day," he marvelled quietly.

"Definitely," she said, extinguishing the stove.

"The way the sun touches the trees – wait, who's that—"

Darcy's ears pricked up and she looked up, turning her head to the window.

There was nothing there, but Roman was looking at her.

Watching her.

He smiled slyly. "My mistake," he whispered. "A trick of the light."

Darcy swallowed.

"Enjoy your tea," Roman said calmly, and he strolled back across the kitchen and disappeared into the hall.

Henry ducked a branch and slipped between two tall beech trees, their trunks beautifully white and peeling into curls, sunlight brushing tendrils and flakes of bark with gold. The leaves above her were a bright, brilliant green, spattered with orange. Dead matter crunched beneath her heels.

The woods were quiet here, and though she had not ventured too deep inside she felt that the world beyond the trees had been snatched away from her entirely. Her mind wandered toward thoughts of home…

Then wandered away again. Something at the back of her skull, some tiny voice, edged her memories out of reach, and she moved on. She frowned for a moment, confused. The voice was barely audible, a whisper rather than anything substantial, and yet… it felt as though it had come from somewhere external.

Like something had detected her reaching for her memories and kicked away her hand.

She shook off the ridiculous thought and pushed on, gripping her hunting rifle with both hands. It was crooked against her waist, the stock buried in her hip, the barrel aimed steadily at the root system of each tree she passed. No sense in lifting it high and wasting her energy; when she needed it, she thought, she would like to have some feeling left in her arms.

"Somewhere to hide," she whispered. She had been walking for twenty minutes or so, largely moving in circles, trying to stay close to the edge of the forest. This made hiding difficult, however, for the trees were thin here. Deciding that deeper meant thicker, and thicker meant more places to burrow herself away, she pushed inward.

An hour or two. That was all.

Half a mile or so deeper, she crunched into a small clearing and saw a knot of tangled shrubbery snaking between three or four trees. Large, thorny thickets burst out of the ground and wound around each other, forming a scaffolding for a thick blanket of ivy. "Perfect," Henry said, stepping into the clearing and crossing it quickly. Slinging the rifle onto her back, she ducked into the thorns.

She winced as sharp needles dragged across her forehead and cheeks, tiny beads of blood forming in the grazes. Dipping her head low, she crawled into the thicket and found a small hollow. Dropping the rifle to the ground, she perched on her rump and looked out. She could hardly see into the clearing anymore through the thick branches, and was fairly confident that nothing would be able to see her either.

What the hell kind of exotic animals had Roman

procured, anyway?

Christ, were there *lions* out here? She had been so concerned with the fact that there might be slithering, fleshy abominations like the kind she had killed the night before that she had forgotten the danger of Big Game: what kind of animals did these rich fuckers usually come out here to kill? Tigers? Rhino?

Or did 'exotic' mean 'people'? Was that what Wayne Roman's weekend gathering was really about?

Henry sat for a while, occasionally rearing up her head and peering out through the thorns. Eventually she began to feel exposed, more and more sunlight poking into her hidey-hole as the morning passed. Speckles and points of grey light splashed the thickets, and the low carpet of mist at her feet became a broiling, angry white. She became uncomfortable after half an hour or so, and moved into a crouch so that she could reposition herself a little deeper in the overgrowth—

She froze as a dead branch cracked somewhere behind her.

Henry crouched perfectly still, paused awkwardly mid-adjustment so that, after just a few seconds, her back began to ache. She hardly noticed; she was watching through the thorns out of the very corner of her eye.

For a moment there was absolute silence. No birdsong – she had noticed that earlier – and not a sliver of sound otherwise.

Then another *crunch*, and her heart smacked the inside of her ribcage.

Gently she moved her head, confident that if she strained her neck any further the thing behind her would hear the bones creaking. Gently, gently…

A shadow watched her from outside the thorns.

Henry's hand shot to her mouth and she clamped her palm over the scream that threatened to escape. Wide-eyed she watched as the shadow – an indiscernible shape somewhere in the trees, a dozen feet from her – less – heaved, its body quivering with long, silent breaths.

Her eyes stung. *Don't*, she warned herself sternly, don't scream, don't cry, don't *breathe*…

The thing's shoulders rolled forward. It hunched, ready to pounce, its eyes on her. Slowly, gingerly, she reached for the rifle.

A shadow flitted behind her. Reeling, she snapped her head around to look, but the shadow had gone already. She turned back—

The original shape was gone.

A *crack* back in the clearing.

Henry whimpered, grabbed desperately at the gun – fumbled, missed it – finally found it and wound her fingers around the barrel, dragging the thing toward her. Another shadow slunk past on her left and she cringed, cowering into herself. Christ, there were three of them. At least three. Were lions pack animals?

No, she knew that these weren't lions. She had seen the thing – only vaguely, but she had seen its *size* – and knew that lions didn't get that big.

These were monsters.

Henry shifted the rifle into her waist and swung it gently, wincing as dangling thorns moved around her. Something lurched past her on the right – that was *four* – and she aimed the weapon into the clearing.

Bright eyes shone yellow, pinned on her, hungry and delighted at the opportunity for a hunt.

Henry drew in a deep breath and laid her finger on the trigger.

The creature lowered its head, stalking slowly forward. Behind her another *crunch* as the second beast moved closer. She was trapped, surrounded, already calculating reload time as she prepared to fire—

Somewhere in the forest, somebody screamed.

The creature in the clearing lifted its head, shadowy body extending as those yellow eyes rose out of Henry's line of sight. There was a dreadful, insect-like clicking sound behind her, followed moments later by a similar series of squeaks and rattles off to her right. The creatures were communicating.

With a great *thwump*, the beast in the clearing thundered out through the trees, the others following. Henry was suddenly left alone, gripping the rifle with white knuckles, head pounding.

Finally, when she was certain they'd gone, she started breathing again.

7:

LIGHTNING

Eliza Barron moved quietly through the trees, dark trousers already spattered with muck. Her height became a disadvantage and she found herself ducking beneath overhanging branches, peering into the shadows half-aware that anything out there would quite easily be able to spot her in the thick undergrowth.

She had hardly spoken to any of the other guests, though she felt that she'd managed to accurately discern most of their characters from the brief snippets of conversation she had heard. Greedy rich bastards, all of them. The idea of the hunt repulsed her, even more so now that she had encountered that twisted hybrid-thing that Roman had encouraged them all to shoot in the ballroom.

But she wasn't here for the hunt.

Listening carefully, she moved slowly forward with

the rifle grasped awkwardly in both hands. She was more convinced than ever now that she'd been right: Roman was at the bottom of all this, and he would—

A branch snapped somewhere to her right.

Eliza swung her rifle around, snapping the bolt forward with a loud *snick* and pressing one eye closed as she pointed it into the trees. The dawn-light was settling now and it had become somewhat easier to see into the pines, though every shadow still swelled with the lingering cloak of night that had covered them previously.

For a moment she stood entirely still, squinting hard into the trees. When it became apparent that the sound had been little more than the movements of a squirrel, or perhaps a badger slipping back to its set, she lowered the gun and prepared to move on.

Something moved, off to her left this time.

Eliza drew in a sharp breath and lifted the rifle, her head snapping around so violently that she nearly missed it: a shape in the trees, small and lithe but moving awkwardly, barrelling toward her.

She laid her finger on the trigger and slammed the butt of the rifle into her shoulder. The creature kept coming, branches snapping under its feet as it cast odd shadows on the trees. Eliza Barron took a deep breath, steadied herself. "Come on then, you—"

The shape staggered into view.

Eliza lowered the rifle hastily, only realising now

that her heart had begun to pump twice its normal speed. "Goodness, young lady, I almost had you!"

Henrietta Heller raised both hands as she clocked the weapon, slowing to a breathless stop. "I heard screaming," she panted. "Creatures – out there – I don't know what—"

"Slow down," Eliza hissed. "Come here. What are you doing running about like that?"

Henry stumbled over.

"Look at you, poor girl!" the tall woman said. Her voice was a surprise, thicker than Henry had expected. She slung the rifle over her back and started to brush down Henry's blouse, flakes of moss and leaf falling off her. "Goodness."

"You're not like the others, are you?" Henry said quietly, glancing about them. "The hunters. You're different."

Eliza said nothing.

"What are you doing here?" Henry whispered. "You're not here to hunt. You don't seem… well… you don't seem to be enjoying all this."

Eliza shook her head. "Truthfully, child, I'm looking for somebody." Looking furtively into the trees, she seemed to come to a decision. "My husband came to one of Wayne Roman's scientific showcases last year. A night of frivolity and experimentation, he told me. Honestly, he was looking for inspiration."

Shadows moved all around them. Just the swaying,

wind-touched trunks of the trees? Or something else?

"My husband is – *was* – a writer, you see," Eliza continued, her voice hushed. "Tales of horror and excitement. He thought one of Roman's infamous showcases would be the perfect fuel for his next story."

"Barron," Henry realised. "The others were talking about him. Spencer Barron."

"He disappeared," Eliza nodded. "My husband never came home. And now that I've seen the kind of abominable creature Roman spends his time creating – oh, what other cursed things must exist in that laboratory of his – I am certain my husband has been killed."

"I'm so sorry," Henry said. She shivered. Roman had exuded such a sickening level of charisma since he had introduced himself, and had convinced the others that he was some kind of pioneer, some figure of achievement… he was a crook, she had known it from the moment he led them into the ballroom. But just how crooked? "We'll get him," she said confidently.

"Roman's going to pay, you can be certain of that, child. But if I have any hope of finding my husband…"

Henry nodded. Her thoughts flashed to Darcy, waiting for her back at the house. For a moment she wanted to run back there, to find the maid – Roman's adopted daughter; surely she couldn't be as wicked as her guardian – and get away from here. They could run away together. Perhaps Darcy wanted to get out of here as much as she did…

Perhaps they could find somewhere to stay together. Just for a while. Away from Henry's parents, from Roman…

But that was selfish. And stupid. Now wasn't the time for fancies. To think somebody might actually have been *killed*… "I'll help you," Henry said, reaching for her father's single-shot. "Two heads are better than one, right?"

"You're a kind girl," Eliza nodded. "Let's see what's out there."

Together they marched through the woods for a time, dry leaves crunching beneath their feet. Above them the first real touches of sunlight sprayed into the canopy. Henry felt oddly safe with the woman, especially knowing that she wasn't here to hunt. And though the circumstances of her presence were unfortunate, she was glad that Eliza was here.

"This scientific showcase," Henry said, "what was he showcasing? Roman, I mean."

Eliza sighed. "All sorts of things, really. From what I know, at least. I never found out what my husband saw, of course, but I've heard things. Our fellow hunters – the brothers in uniform? – seem to have attended a few of these gatherings."

She swept her rifle softly left and right, her eyes moving between trees as though she suspected every trunk to begin moving suddenly and clamp its predatory branches around them.

"I believe he began by experimenting with electricity," Eliza said. "'Wayne Roman's famous lightning displays'… he would generate miniature storms, I believe, and illuminate his visitors with wild tornadoes of indoor electricity. Then the electricity turned to fire, and the fire became poisons, and gases, and great glass balls of oceanic life… and then the madness increased. Soon he was parading creatures before his guests, awful hybrids: things, I imagine, rather like the creature we saw last night. Human-animal hybrids, suffering pets made from dead and dying things… innocent, except in their blasphemous existence."

"Is that what's out here with us?" Henry whispered. "More of those… things?"

Eliza turned to her, smiling weakly. Her rifle lowered slowly. "Whatever's out here, you're safe with me. I'll make sure of that, sweetheart—"

There was a great dry *crunch* in the canopy above them and something slopped out of the branches, a titanic pair of moss-covered jaws opening wide and slamming shut around the top half of Eliza Barron's body. Henry screamed, staggering back as the creature's teeth sheared through meat and bone with ease and sprayed red mist into the earth.

The beast was enormous, snake-like, but instead of scales its flesh was like dry earth, thick clouds of moss and blue mould blossoming across its skin. The creature's vast, semi-reptilian neck plunged out of the canopy, bulging as the thing's jaws worked to chew through Eliza's waist; Henry glanced up and saw that the its body wound through the tops of dozens of trees, impossibly long and thick, rippling with dry green scales – yes, it did have scales, she saw, but they were like stone – and clumps of fuzz-green lichen.

Before Henry could fire off a shot the thing had whipped upward again, ripping half of Eliza with it. It tipped its head back and threw Eliza's torso and head back into its throat, great ropes of blood swinging out of its mossy lips. Teeth flashed as it crunched loudly, then it turned its head toward Henry again and hissed. A colossal blue tongue flitted between curved, white fangs the length of Henry's body.

Eliza's legs stood in the undergrowth for a minute, blood spurting from the stump of her waist as frayed ribbons of meat wriggled, recently oxygenated for the first time. Cartilage shone where the woman's upper half had been and the earth between her feet was soaked red.

Henry screamed as Eliza's legs swayed forward and flopped into the earth. The creature swallowed, bright red viscera hanging from its reptilian jaws as its eyes flared with a hungry blue fire.

Quietly Darcy crossed the entrance hall, padding softly over the tiles.

Her fingers brushed the doorknob and she glanced behind her, frightened that she'd been followed. For an hour now she had waited, watching through the windows in the kitchen and from the servants' quarters. There was no sign of Henry. Something had happened.

There was a muffled *click* as the knob twisted and she pushed the front door open.

Stepping out onto the doorstep, she raised a hand to shield her eyes from the sun and looked out toward the trees. The forest was still, the treetops barely touched by a soft wind; no sign of anybody – or anything – inside.

"Come on," she whispered. "Where are you…?"

A hand clapped down on her shoulder.

Darcy jolted. Thick dark-skinned fingers squeezed the muscle of her shoulder, hard, and she looked up.

Wayne Roman towered above her, smiling thinly.

"I wasn't…" Darcy whispered. "I didn't—"

"Let's get you inside, shall we?" Roman said darkly. Glancing toward the trees, he clenched his jaws. His eyes bristled with anger. "It's cold out here."

With that he grabbed her arm roughly and yanked her inside, the great oak doors slamming behind them.

8:
JELLY AND GUNPOWDER

Chaos exploded into the trees as Oswald Heller squeezed the trigger of his 54, the blast kicking back hard into the meat of his shoulder.

"What is it?" Mary Gilmour hissed, elbowing her husband in the ribs.

Cavan shook his head. "I saw it a moment ago… balls, where's the blasted thing gone?"

"I reckon I got him," Oswald said, reloading his rifle as he stepped forward. "Let me go fetch the bastard."

"Wait—"

Something leapt down from the branches onto Oswald's shoulders, a blur of globular white. Oswald recoiled, wheeling around quickly and looking up into the trees. Already the thing was crawling onto his skull and he yelped, swinging the rifle and smacking the thing in what he imagined was its head. The creature was knocked loose with a wet *splurt* and flew into the dirt at his feet.

"What the devil..."

The creature looked up and shrieked, a piercing whine coming from somewhere within its gelatinous body. Before Oswald could move it had leapt onto his belly and it scrambled around his body and beneath his armpit, scuttling up his back. He cried out as it appeared again at his neck, latching onto him and plunging one clawed hand into his cheek. Blood winged from his mouth as the flesh of his face was ripped open and the creature suckered its belly to the back of his head, enveloping his skull and sucking at the wound.

Alicia Heller screamed.

The report of another shot echoed through the trees and Cavan's rifle smouldered, the thick stench of blown gunpowder blooming around them. "Another one!" he yelled, swinging the rifle around as a second creature leapt out of the trees, its flesh bright white and rubbery. It was only the size of a badger or fox, but round and gelatinous, its eyes no more than deep black pits in what could hardly pass for a face. In fact no part of the creature's body seemed to have been moulded into anything recognisable: its arms were shifting tendrils of jelly-like white flesh that lengthened and contracted as it writhed, its mouth a shallow dent in the wet mess of its... stomach? Yet, there were teeth, flashing one moment and withdrawing into gluey gums the next. The creature seemed to blur and clarify, solid one moment then rubbery and loose the next.

It was a demon.

Alicia screamed again as a third of the insane things dropped from the sky and landed on her chest, blobby tentacles exploding from it and suckering to her clothes. Before she could raise an arm, a fourth creature had burst out of the earth at her feet and latched onto her calf; she felt needle-like things piercing her skin and the heady sensation of something being drained from her. More of them – one to her left, another slithering down the trunk of a tree across the clearing – and the scream died in her throat as something slipped into her mouth, something that tasted like liquorice and was tinged with the metallic, awful tang of blood.

"They're everywhere!" Mary Gilmour moaned, firing her rifle into another of the things as more came from the trees. The creature exploded into thick strings of white goop, sprayed open by shot, then seemed to suck itself back into shape. The shot was sucked in too, and where the creature had been a creamy white before it was now speckled with black and brown. Beside her Cavan yowled in agony as another consumed his arm, clamping onto his hand and firing its limbs upward, tentacles of white mucus shooting up toward his shoulder and quickly disabling him.

A cacophony of shrieking and ripping and wet, sloppy tearing filled the forest as the creatures descended, dozens of them, each as hungry as the last.

The shadows flitted past Henry in a blur of red and green as she tumbled through the forest, her heart pounding in her chest. She could hear them all around her now: creatures stalking the canopy above her; more slinking through the branches on their way down to the dirt. Wide snouts yawed open in the half-light of the dawn as great shapes lurched toward her from deep within the forest. Behind her the titanic snake hissed again, the vicious sound booming into her skull.

Henry yelled as her toes slid beneath a protruding white root, twisting over on her ankle and sprawling in the dirt. Dead leaves bloomed around her as she fell heavily into the earth and a flash of heat hammered into her nose. Blood drizzled onto her lip. A hot white bolt of pain shot up her leg as she tried to wrench it free of the root's grasp. The rifle had fallen into the dirt and a cloud of dead leaves bloomed around it, just out of reach.

Above her, the snake slithered forward.

She glanced up, eyes widening as she saw the enormous beast moving through the canopy. Its body was looped around four or five trees, its tail swinging slowly behind it, its eyes flaring with icy blue heat.

Desperately she grabbed her leg and pulled, but the root held fast. The snake advanced—

"Fuck!" she yelled, twisting her leg hard. There was a wet *crunch* and the root snapped, freeing her violently and throwing her onto her stomach. An enormous creak sounded overhead as the giant, moss-covered snake expanded from the trees open-mouthed and she felt the tip of its flitting tongue brush the top of her head; scrambling forward, she lurched over another root and tumbled into the trees. Behind her the snake's jaws snapped shut. She looked back desperately over her shoulder and saw the gun in the dirt – too far away now – and, cursing her empty hands, she abandoned it and darted into the shadows.

Henry ran, zigzagging wildly, stupidly disoriented. Which way was the estate? Eliza was gone and she had no hope of finding her family out here, not without shouting and giving herself away; there was no option but to run for the house and hope that Darcy was there to let her in.

Somewhere in the woods she heard a scream, followed by the triumphant, guttural bellow of another creature. Another like the one that had dropped out of the trees and bitten Eliza Barron in half? Or were there others out here?

Henry heaved herself to her feet and staggered forward, half-falling through the trees and reaching out to steady herself. Her hand grazed something solid and sharp and she looked down. Dust fell through her fingers as she moved her hand. She had grabbed something non-organic and for a moment the sensation was incredible; when her head had stopped pounding, she realised what she was looking at.

The earth around her was scattered with crumbling stone and debris. Here, jutting out of the ground and leaning into a cluster of roots, was something that looked like the top of a small, broken wall. The brickwork itself was obscured by thick layers of blue, fuzzy lichen but too angular in shape to be anything natural; was there some kind of building around here?

The exploded wall continued east, vaguely so at least, rolling up and down as entire sections spilled into the overgrowth. Following the wall with hazy clouds of black at the edges of her vision, mania pumping through her blood, Henry staggered into another clearing and marvelled at the wreckage of a small building half-hidden in the trees. She had found the icehouse, she realised, little more than a narrow, rectangular black hole in the earth. The outer walls of the building were covered in ivy and thick, bulging clumps of moss. Cracked tiles and limestone bricks were scattered about the mouth of the ancient structure.

She remembered what Roman had said:

Just don't go in the icehou—

"Oh, fuck that," Henry whispered, staggering forward and into the dark.

PART THREE

BASEMENT MACHINES

9:
THE BEAST

"You can't keep me in here!" Darcy yelled, wrestling the doorknob with both hands. The door wouldn't budge; he had locked it from the outside. She slammed a hand on the wood panelling. It stung. "You can't!"

Fuming, she backed away from the door. She had grown up in this bedroom. it was large, with maroon walls and a tall dormer looking out onto the front lawn and the woods beyond. He hadn't bothered telling her not to watch out the window. He *wanted* her to see. To look on helplessly, unable to do anything, as Henry emerged from the woods and ran to the place Darcy had told her to come. To watch as Roman met her there instead. And then what? Would he send her back into the woods? Or worse…

"Let me out!" Darcy screamed, barrelling back into the door and pounding with both fists. Behind her dappled light filtered onto the luxurious sheets covering a deep four-poster bed, the oak frame carved intricately with designs that she had memorised over the years. On one post wad depicted a great battle between Cavalier and Roundhead forces during the English Civil War, every soldier and plume of smoke carved out of the wood in glorious detail, blood and severed limbs spilling and spiralling downward. On another, the aftermath: a mound of bodies winding up the oak, smouldering and useless. Cut into the bedframe were monstrous gargoyle-like faces and images of Hell and war. As a child she had been nonplussed, hardly paying attention to them. Then she had looked, and kept looking, and for a long time she had slept uneasily.

She still did.

"Let me out of here!"

Darcy stopped, exhausted, panting. Her fists hurt from smacking the door and her arms were tired. There was nobody out on the landing, nobody listening. Roman was downstairs somewhere – probably in the basement laboratory, if anything, and much too far away to hear her. He had done this before, whenever she spoke out of turn or questioned him in a fashion he didn't appreciate. She had been locked in this room, in fact, more times than she could count.

Outside the hunt continued.

Darcy walked limply across her bedroom to the dormer, laying one hand on the glass and looking out into the forest. She had heard screams, minutes ago, and occasionally there was the shriek of some mad creature, or the clicking, chirruping calls of others communicating across the clearings. During the night she had heard, more than once, the long, low roar of something enormous and beastly.

"Where are you…?" she whispered. Her breath fogged up the glass.

Movement downstairs.

Darcy turned her head, looking past the bed and her dresser to the bedroom door. She listened for a moment, then heard it again: shuffling sounds in the entrance hall below.

The footsteps continued, limping and dragging footsteps, as something moved across the tiles. Darcy hurried across the room and pounded on the door again. "Dad?" she yelled. "Dad? Roman? Is that you, will you let me out now? Please?"

Hammering on the oak, she sobbed:

"Dad, I'm sorry! I'm sorry, okay? Please, come let me out—"

Relief flooded her as the shuffling footsteps began to grow closer. Climbing up the stairs toward her.

She staggered back from the door. "Oh, thank you, thank you so much… I'll be good," she called, "I promise I'll…"

Something slopped onto the landing outside and she hesitated. Her eyes dropped to the bottom of the door.

A tiny slit of light bled through, a wedge of flickering amber that pervaded the pool of shadows at the very edge of the room. the gas lamps on the landing burned softly, calmly, their soft glow a physical antithesis to the mania fuelling her pumping heart. Too fast, too loud. It was outside the door now—

Her breath hitched in her throat as a shadow fell heavily into the slot of light and blotted it out. The smell had reached her now, a smell like putrid meat, fruity and colourful and awful. The thing out there wasn't Roman, and it hadn't come to let her out.

"Dad?" she whispered hopefully.

Something snarled quietly outside the door. Right outside, its muzzle pressed to the wood. The way its shadow moved, oozing left and right, was inhuman and terrible. Darcy took a step back.

The floorboards moaned loudly beneath her feet. Darcy cringed, frozen still.

Too late.

The creature bumped its snout against the door, poking it almost softly. The snarling was hungry and wet now. Darcy's breath was clamped in her chest, the ribs vice-like, her heart struggling. It was there, right there, it could smell her…

Darcy took another step back and the floor screamed.

The creature's snarling became lustful and hot and it bumped the door again, hard enough this time to rattle the wood in its frame. Darcy looked all around, searching the room desperately for a weapon or something she could throw.

The door rattled again.

"Dad!" she called, frightened now, hoping that he was down there somewhere.

The creature growled.

"Oh God…" Darcy breathed.

It would go, she thought. If she just waited a moment, it would forget she was in here. It would leave. She counted, holding her breath: *Five. Four. Three. Two—*

The door exploded inward and Darcy staggered back as it slammed onto the floor in a great cloud of dust and wooden shards. The creature bellowed in the debris-filled doorway.

Its eyes fell on her and she screamed.

Ronald Harcourt yelled as the beast wheeled around and charged toward them, its great paws punching hard into the earth and scattering clouds of dead and blood-spattered material. It moved frighteningly fast: in less than a second it had crossed the clearing.

"What the bloody fuck is that?" Lou roared, raising his Berthier and preparing to fire.

There was a sound like branches breaking as a set of gnarled, bony claws slid out of its paw and slammed into Lou's chest, throwing him back into a tree before Ronnie could even lift his own rifle.

"Leave him!" Ronnie yelled, frantically firing a shot in the creature's direction. The clap of the rifle drew the beast's attention as the bullet smacked the belly of a tree across the clearing, chunks of wood exploding into the earth. The monster bellowed, a trio of shining yellow lights blazing hatefully in its skull as it turned on him. Three hungry eyes blinked at once, leathery lids closing then slicing open again. It smiled.

Lou gasped for breath as the creature withdrew its paw, blood winging from his chest as the claws slid out of his flesh. His body slid heavily down the tree with a groan and he heaved in the dirt as Ronnie tried desperately to reload his rifle, his eyes flitting from the weapon to the beast turning toward him.

Shoulders hunched, the bony armoured segments of the bear-sized thing drew back as its spines quivered.

Its maw opened into a terrifying grin and it pounced.

Ronnie felt bolts of pain splintering his side and stomach as the thing's massive paws blew him back into the clearing. Then it was on top of him, strings of wet, bloody slaver swinging in his face as hot, ripe breath blasted him. The beast's eyes burned like fire in the hollow pits of its grimacing exoskeletal mask and he screamed. He was looking into the face of the devil itself, and it was hungry.

There was an explosion of sound and the creature's

shoulder ruptured, chunks of bone flying as meaty tendrils of viscera sprung from the wound. Across the clearing Louis Harcourt was frantically reloading his Berthier, four red teardrops spreading across his chest even as he moved.

The beast didn't seem to notice.

Ronnie's screams died in his mouth in a wet slop of red as the creature clamped its jaws around his neck and ripped it open, yanking half his spine out through his throat. His vision swam; something had burst in his chest with the weight of the creature straddling him. His ribs were broken.

In the last, bloody second before it all went black, Ronnie helplessly watched as another of the things slunk out of the shadows and started to creep toward his brother.

The abomination slithered into Darcy's room, a nightmare of melded flesh and copper with the face of a dead man. Darcy shrieked as it scuttled over the toppled door, punching its spider-like arms into the wood and ripping chunks of wood free. it hissed as it moved forward, its belly dragging over the floor as a dozen metallic limbs skittered behind it.

"Get out!" Darcy screamed, backing up against the nearest bedpost. *"Get out!"*

The creature had a grotesque, bulbous abdomen

coated in some kind of slick, pulpy membrane. It drizzled on the floor, pulsing and throbbing awfully. Its midsection was cradled in a rusted metal belt, and clicking metal legs thrust out of its meaty body, attached by mechanical pistons and cables. It was a hybrid of muscle and metal, a sick amalgamation of parts organic and otherwise. It was staring at her with emotionless, drooping eyes, its face stitched on with copper wire, its mouth pinned open with staples. Inside, a row of vicious metal teeth champed hungrily behind a set of broken real dentures.

The thing lunged and Darcy ducked beneath a swinging brass pincer, still screaming as it whistled over her head. A series of clicks boomed from the thing's underbelly as she darted to the left and it wheeled around, its eyes locked on her. Only now did she notice the segmented tail exploding from the thing's back, and her eyes widened as it flashed toward her. She tumbled into the wall as it glanced off her shoulder, smacking bone before punching into the plaster by her ear.

The creature scuttled forward, twice her size and drooling spittle and oil. Another metal arm lashed out and this one caught her in the stomach, grazing her belly and leaving a bright spot of pain throbbing across her flesh. She shrieked and rushed for the door, stumbling over another snapping leg and nearly falling onto her face. The creature skittered after her, skidding madly over its own legs as its tail whipped into the nearest bedpost and smashed it open. Wood flew into the window and glass sprayed into the morning-light, dancing in a gold whirlwind of tiny pieces. The four-poster groaned and sunk with an almighty bellow of wood, the mattress flattened by a plummeting slab of marbled oak. Down exploded into the room in a blossom of white fluff.

A spinning copper pike smashed into Darcy's calf and she yelled in agony as she sprawled onto her stomach, crawling madly through the doorway and out onto the landing. Tears streamed down her face and she turned onto her back, fumbling for a splinter of wood. The creature loomed over her, its eyes blank and cold, its throat clicking and ripping open as brassy pins and pistons worked the surgically-implanted teeth. It grinned, raising two mechanical legs far above its head.

The report of a pistol shattered Darcy's eardrum and she smelled smoke before she registered the wall of pulpy tissue that had splashed her face. She moaned, blood drizzling into her mouth. A weight slammed into the landing beside her and she looked down at the creature's head, turned inside-out and pooling into the carpet. Its metal legs bucked and convulsed as death throes pulsed through the creature's body.

Roman stood over them both, the gun smouldering in his hand.

His teeth were gritted, his eyes seething with the same smoke that rolled out of the pistol's barrel. "Get up," he whispered.

"What is this thing?" Darcy croaked. "Is this one of yours? Or one of—"

"Enough," Roman said. "Get up. Now."

"No," Darcy said through tears. "Go away. Leave me here. Please."

Roman sighed. Pinched the bridge of his nose and took a deep breath. Then he raised the gun and pointed it between Darcy's eyes. "Up," he said simply.

Darcy raised her hands, struggling to her feet. "This is monstrous," she breathed. "All of it. The hunt – your experiments… I can't live here anymore. I can't be a part of this."

Roman smiled thinly. "You've never had a problem with it before."

"It's getting worse," Darcy seethed. The hands raised over her head trembled as she spoke. "You've gone too far."

"It's the girl, isn't it?" Roman said. He laughed smugly. "It is. Oh, that's beautiful. *Henrietta.* You know, she wasn't on the list. I don't know why those two *fucks* thought it would be a good idea to bring her."

His smile faded.

"And it's certainly backfired now, hasn't it?"

Darcy swallowed. Said nothing.

"You *like* her, don't you?"

Beside her the creature's body twitched one last time, then fell still. The sound of the shot was still ringing in Darcy's ears.

"Disgusting," Roman spat. He cocked the gun. "Come on."

"No."

Then the barrel jabbed her forehead, hard, and he leaned in. "Come with me," he insisted. "Or you'll see how *he* feels."

10 (*INTERLUDE*):
MOONDISC

While the forest screamed, *it* listened.

On the mantelpiece of a room full of insanities, a room in the home of a madman, it sat inside a glass canister seething.

Where had it come from?

It was called the *Moondisc* and for all the world it looked just like a sliver shaved from the surface of the moon itself, a bowl-shaped hunk of that constantly orbiting satellite. An impossibility on a thin metal stand, catching all the light that speckled the outside of its bell-shaped cage and reflecting it back:

Wherever it had come from, the Moondisc *shone*.

Its surface was imperfect and flecked with microscopic chips, infinitesimally small shadows gathering in shallow pools across the outer edges. Those edges were rough-hewn and splintered like the many-toothed edge of a saw had carelessly gouged away the rest of this strange object. It was a delicately organic white colour, marbled stripes and whorls of creamy yellow pooling faintly through it; in this room of masks and spears and statues, it was almost entirely insignificant. Unnoticeable. And yet it had pride of place on the mantelpiece, right in the centre.

Listening.

11:

WHO? SAID THE RICH CUNT

Mary Gilmour staggered back into the middle of the clearing, gripping her rifle in one hand and wiping stinking white goop off her mouth with the other. She bumped into something and yelped, wheeling around with the weapon raised.

"Don't shoot me," Cavan yelled, his arm entirely enveloped in the elongated, stretching body of one of the gelatinous white creatures. "Get it off!"

Mary reacted on instinct, pointing the rifle at her husband's elbow and squeezing the trigger.

Cavan screamed, his arm exploding in a pulp of white and pink. The creature hissed as it was blown into the trees, separating into sticky strands of jelly and smacking the trunks with a wet *pop* before drizzling down them into the earth. Hunks of meat followed, Cavan's arm shattering and spraying the foliage. The *crack* of bone that immediately succeeded the clap of the rifle was deafening, but all of this was drowned out by the man's agonised shrieking. He crumpled to his knees and Mary stared in awe as blood swung out of the stump of his shoulder, still flecked with gunk, in thick red walls.

His mouth was still open and screeching when another of the creatures flopped out of the canopy above and ballooned over his head, muffling the sound. It squirmed and twitched, tiny tentacles lashing out of its wet, raw body as Cavan tried to shake it off. He reached up with his good arm and clawed wildly at the thing as another plopped onto his back. Mary Gilmour heard teeth sliding into his flesh and the awful sounds of chewing. Blood started running down his neck and onto his chest in runnels; the creature enveloping his head had sunk its tiny sucker-teeth into his throat.

Still running on mania and terror, Mary raised the rifle again and pointed it at her husband's head.

Behind them, Alicia Heller was overcome with tiny white bodies. Gripping the creature latched onto her chest with both hands, she tried desperately to wrench it off as another attacked her calf. Her mouth was full of jelly and she spat, gobs of white flying out with her spittle. Something attached to her shoulder poked at her lips with another tentacle and she bit down, hard, the awful taste of liquorice filling her windpipe. The thing flailed, fell, and finally she tore away the thing on her chest, screaming as a ring of hot wet points pulsed across her sternum. Where the thing had dug in its teeth, blood beaded and pooled over the fabric of her hunting dress. She threw the creature into the dirt at her feet and stamped. The thing on her calf screeched as it was shaken loose and flecked with the chunks of its crushed sibling; before she could celebrate her victory, another pair had dropped from the trees onto her arms and the one on her shoulder had slipped its tentacle into her ear.

More were dropping all around them, plopping into the dirt one by one, fifty or so of the wretched things – forget it, sixty; eighty now – and Oswald Heller turned a violent circle, pumping loud shots into the edges of the clearing. White shapes erupted into showers of spittle-like fluid and the clearing was filled with the smell of spent gunpowder and sugar.

A loud report filled the forest and Oswald looked across the clearing to see Cavan Gilmour's head blown off his body in a spray of red and white. His headless body fell onto its back in the dirt and dead leaves and before more than a second the creatures had descended on it like carrion birds to roadkill. Oswald's eyes widened. The creatures covered the corpse within moments, their malleable bodies joining, melting into each other, becoming one shape, a thick coating that spread and seeped all around the carcass, a shell of jelly...

Cavan started to twitch. To move. And Oswald

realised that the creatures had become one, an exosuit of shining white horror compelling Cavan's corpse to rise onto its knees and single hand, then to stand straight—

Mary Gilmour shrieked as more of the creatures slammed into her chest and stomach, propelling her onto her back in the dirt. The gun dropped uselessly to the ground as another swung down onto her shoulder and squeezed around her upper arm, tightening so violently that her fingers flexed open. God, they were filling her mouth, her nostrils, spilling into her eyes…

"Help me!" Alicia yelled, and Oswald recoiled, spinning around and raising his weapon. The jerking, slopping Cavan-thing lurched toward him and Oswald swung the butt of the rifle into the amalgam's chest, knocking it back a step. Alicia was overcome with a dozen of the creatures, stumbling back into the nearest tree and slamming her back into the wood. There was an awful *splat* as half the creatures exploded, then she turned and smashed her chest into the trunk, more of them spraying the edge of the clearing. Scrabbling with the rest, she clawed madly and looked, agonised, in Oswald's direction.

He lowered his gun. He could feel them climbing his legs, spreading over his back.

"Henry…" Alicia called across the clearing. A white shape appeared in her hair, twisting its tentacles into her scalp. The Cavan-thing clamped its good hand down on Oswald's shoulder and gelatinous fingers began to crush the bone. "Oz, is she safe? Is Henry safe out here?!"

Alicia sunk to her knees. White gunk filled her mouth and her eyes rolled up in her head.

Oswald frowned. *"Who?"*

Then he felt teeth latching onto the back of his neck. Behind him the creatures had fully overtaken Mary Gilmour and they launched their host into him, wrapping her arms around his stomach.

Before the creature clinging to his arm could take over his fingers, he pointed the rifle up into the meat of his jowls, rammed the barrel hard into the ceiling of his chin, and compressed the trigger.

Louis Harcourt lay panting on the forest floor, blood streaming from a wound on his temple, the rifle empty and abandoned. His chest was shredded, his life pumping steadily from him in thick, glossy ribbons.

Ronnie was dead.

Louis watched helplessly, breathless and exhausted, as one of the armoured bear-creatures nuzzled Ronnie's stomach, scooping ropes of intestine out of the cavity and slopping them down. Its bony mask was smeared with red, eyes flaring through the sockets of the cracked, horned façade. Louis sputtered and it turned its head toward him, grinning red. The second beast was already approaching, padding slowly toward him through the trees. In moments it would pounce and savage him.

"Fuck," Louis whispered pointlessly.

The blood-covered beast turned its body fully and prowled toward him, both of them now moving through the dead leaves and tiny bones with hardly a sound. In fact the forest seemed full of his own laboured breathing and the bubbling of blood in his throat; he even fancied he could hear the faint wheeze of his lungs deflating.

Louis had almost resigned himself completely when there was a hissing sound above him.

One of the great beasts looked up, its shoulders rolling into the spiny armoured pads of bone clamped to its flesh. It growled angrily, throat smouldering, and Louis followed its gaze up into the treetops.

Narrow reptilian eyes blinked down at him. His heart, weak as it was, fluttered with terror.

The canopy moved and Louis realised he wasn't looking at the boughs and branches of leaves that he had imagined: the snake was titanic, antediluvian; it was a nightmare of mossy skin and grass-stained scales, a colossus of leaf-coloured flesh that slithered through the canopy like an extension of the trees themselves.

"Dear God," he whispered. Elsewhere, faraway, there was screaming. Gunshots. The snake didn't flinch. Louis returned his attention to the armoured bears and saw that they were closer, fur bristling with hunger and excitement, eyes on his bloody chest and throat. And behind them…

The forest was alive.

"Please," he whispered. "Please, no…"

Between the trees, ghostly figures flickered in and out of existence. Translucent and fleeting, they were hardly visible in the filtered light, but he could make their shapes out clearly enough. Here there was a man in a tattered coat with eyes rolling in the sockets of a burned skull; there was a woman gripping the hand of a blank-faced child, both of them covered in blood. The child had a hole in his stomach the size of a cricket ball, and from it spilled scraps of organ that sizzled in the air and disappeared. There must have been a dozen spectral figures, each one floating a foot or so above the ground, all staring at him—

"Leave me alone!" he moaned.

The ground at his feet exploded and a pale white hand thrust out and grabbed his leg. He screamed as a bald, vampiric shape heaved itself out of the dirt, baring its teeth. the snake hissed again and one of the armoured beasts lowered its head and roared, bellowing so furiously that he felt its breath wash across his face. Another of the vampire-like things erupted from the ground a few feet away, scrabbling madly for him, its hands and face so pale that the spidery veins beneath were a vibrant purple.

"Leave me alone! *LEAVE ME—*"

Wet plopping sounds as jelly-like white shapes dropped out of the trees all around him. One of the ghostly figures flickered out of existence, then blurred into being just inches from his face. The grip on his leg tightened, drawing blood.

"Oh, fu—"

The snake lurched forward.

12:

THE TRUTH

Henrietta Heller paused in the icehouse, the darkness below her consuming.

She had expected to find herself in a small, shadowy chamber, light filtering in through tiny drilled holes in the brickwork. In fact she had almost resigned herself to hiding out in here until, inevitably, the snake-like creature found her and swallowed her whole. But standing in the doorway of the icehouse and peering into the dark, she was surprised to see not a single chamber at all but the entrance to a tunnel. The floor of the icehouse sloped downward, into a great black hole beneath the back wall that swallowed every shred of half-light it could.

Swallowing, she moved forward. Ducking her head, she went below the earth, leaving the icehouse façade behind and heading down the tunnel. The walls were stone, and the patches of moss that scattered it made her shudder. Before she could consider the implications of this place she was running her palms along the walls, unable to see; for the next few minutes she followed a long, dark tunnel that sloped gradually downward, leading her out of the forest.

Light up ahead, and she pressed toward it. The floor was no longer packed earth but cement, uneven and sloppy like puddingstone. The light was stronger to her left, and she followed the tunnel around a bend before coming to a fork. Taking the right – it was brighter that way – she found herself faced with a sharp right turn, then one to the left. A straight tunnel forked again, three ways this time, and she chose the middle path.

The tunnel was a labyrinth.

As she bent around a corner, flickering gaslights illuminated the path before her, faint amber whorls dancing on brickwork walls. She was still descending and knew that there was no way to tell what direction she was facing, but she felt that she was heading back to the house. Was the tunnel taking her directly into Roman's basement? Did the maze spread beneath the whole estate?

There was another dreadful shriek from above ground, muffled through layers of earth and cement, and her heart pounded hard in her ears as she moved cautiously forward. She must be thirty yards below ground by now, she thought, perhaps more.

A gas lamp flared briefly, casting its sickly yellow

shadow onto a pitch-black archway at the end of the tunnel, a well of inky nothing.

Swallowing, Henry pressed on, ignoring an opening to her left and continuing to the end of the tunnel. She paused briefly at the archway, then looked back the way she'd come. Nothing there but blackness.

Drawing in a deep breath, she stepped through into the dark.

There was a hum beneath her feet, as if she'd stepped onto an electrified panel, and she recoiled from it, tumbling back into the tunnel. Already, though, the room ahead of her had begun to come to life, and she watched as patches of illumination flickered into existence to the left and right, pools of greasy light spreading one by one as the cavern fired up. Slowly, she stepped forward again.

Henry passed through the arch and onto the vibrating plate, marvelling at the enormous underground chamber. A bank of dim electric lights flared to life on her right and she watched as ceiling-mounted bulbs swivelled into life, splashing the walls of a wide, circular room. The filaments buzzed loudly and machinery whirred in the walls around her, suddenly deafening and ramping up at an alarming rate as she gaped.

"What the…"

The edges of the room were stacked high with scientific equipment, much of it arranged neatly on rusted shelves. Beakers and vials cluttered a long wooden bench, and a pair of rusted filing cabinets in one corner hung half-open, the drawers screaming over each other, bundles of papers and folders spilling out. The walls themselves were brown and black, smeared with stripes of lead-green. Thick bunches of rubber cable ran down from the ceiling, shivering with energy as they snaked toward a central exhibit, something hideously showcased right in the middle of everything.

He was displayed carefully, deliberately, positioned in a great stone chair as though whoever had left him there had *wanted* her to see this.

She turned and vomited onto the concrete, her stomach heaving suddenly at the sight.

Moments later she returned her attention to the thing in the centre of the laboratory, unable to take her eyes off it.

The writer was hooked up to a network of wires and tubes, many of them buried deep in his exposed chest and neck. He was restrained, his wrists and legs bound to the chair with thick leather straps. At first she thought he must be dead, but then she saw that he was twitching, his eyes closed but the lids fluttering. His fingers rapped the arms of the chair erratically, his stomach spasmodically heaving.

As she walked closer and saw the mess of the back of his head, she remembered the Moondisc. Proudly displayed on Roman's mantelpiece, a shallow bowl of stony white, chipped and dented, porous and organic and… familiar, even then. But now, she understood where it had come from.

She moaned.

The top of Spencer Barron's skull had been removed, sawn off with surgical precision, and his scalp had been peeled back so that the plate of bone could be withdrawn. The brain matter inside was exposed and long, wet needles slid into the twitching, squidgy pink-grey tissue, held firm with staples and stitches. His face ended just above the eyes, where skin and bone encircled the quivering, twitching brain. The eyes were rolled up, his mouth open slightly. Thick cables seemed to be pumping something directly into his brain, a spider's web of wires drilled into the man's head and quivering as something flowed through them.

No. Not *into* his brain, she thought. *Out.*

The writer was dreaming.

"Isn't it wonderful?" came Roman's voice from behind her.

She whirled around, panicking. She hadn't heard him come in; had he been watching her from the shadows of the laboratory this whole time?

As Roman stepped forward he stroked a panel of levers on the wall, raking them downward so that a series of glistening glass pipes lit up behind him, thick pulses of white energy surging upward into the ceiling. Into the earth. "The human imagination," he whispered. "What an incredible thing. To harness that…"

He smiled. It was sickening, the expression of a tyrant drunk on the destruction of his kingdom.

He was ill. Horribly, psychotically ill.

"You didn't make those creatures," Henry realised. "I thought… I thought they were experiments. Like the thing you had us shoot last night. But they… no. Oh, God… you didn't make them at all."

"No," Roman smiled, turning away from the rippling glass cylinders to look back at her. "He did."

The writer twitched in his chair. The cables drilled into his skull seemed to pulse and sway as pure, dreadful psychic energy flowed through them, the thoughts and dreams of a man who had only ever created nightmares. Eliza Barron's husband, missing presumed dead… down here all this time, the source of Wayne Roman's most twisted experiment. He had come here so that Roman's insane science could fuel his inspiration – now, it seemed, his imagination was fuelling Roman's work.

"His books were always so… colourful," Roman said, almost dreamily. "Such disturbing creations. Such a brilliant mind, *wasted* on fiction. Much better spent, I think, on creating a reality of his own."

"This is sick," Henry breathed, her stomach churning as she thought of the Moondisc again. Sitting far above them, separated from this man by fifty yards of dirt and the casing of the bell jar. A sliver of his skull, kept above ground to… to what? To focus the creative energy that was being sucked out of the writer's mind? Or simply to remind Roman of his conquest?

Another trophy, that was all. That was all anything was to him.

That was all she was about to be. "You're *sick*."

"Maybe. But what d'you think?" Roman said softly, stepping up beside Barron's chair and laying a hand on the poor writer's arm. He grinned wickedly as somebody screamed far above them. "Am I onto something, Henrietta?"

The writer convulsed gently in his chair. Above ground, the long, triumphant bellow of one of his creatures rang out like a ship's horn, the guttural growl pulsing through the dirt. The sound of something sated.

The hunt was over.

13:

THE TRUTH (II)

Darcy struggled against her ropes, gritting her teeth with frustration.

She was tied to an old pine chair in the kitchen, hands snapped so violently behind her back that her shoulders had begun to ache after ten minutes; her ankles and calves were strapped to the legs of the chair and her rump was sore. She had been wriggling for half an hour. "Come on," she whispered, "come on…"

Beneath her the tiles rattled, the entire floor of the manor house pummelled by some brutish wave of energy below the ground. The kitchen vibrated around her, brass pans swinging loudly on their hooks. Somewhere in the house an ornament was knocked from the rumbling mantelpiece and she heard glass shatter on the floor. Roman's basement machines usually caused murmurations through the building but never to this degree: there was something going on down there, something awful…

"Come *on*," she hissed. Outside the house there was a mighty bellow and she winced, not daring to look toward the window. She tugged at and wrestled with the ropes, wrists sore and burned, her arms aching from the effort. It was no good. Her whole upper body was straining now as she tried to work the ropes loose, the chair legs rocking on the uneven floor and threatening to tip her over. With an enormous grunt she tried one last time to wrench both of her hands free—

No good. No good. She was stuck here…

Somewhere, there was a scream.

Darcy's eyes widened. She looked up at the ceiling, drawing in a deep breath. She had one option left, one that she'd been avoiding, but if somebody was in danger out there…

"Help me God," she breathed. Then she grabbed her left hand with the trembling fingers of the right and jammed her wrist into the back of the chair. Holding her breath, she counted to three

(*don't don't don't*)

then, with a pre-emptive yelp, violently twisted her body.

The yelp turned into a scream as a sick, dry *crack* boomed behind her and a bolt of agony shot up her arm. The rope slipped easily off her broken left wrist, then the loosened knot slid lazily off her right. Still moaning with pain, she brought her arms around to her chest and clutched her left desperately. Her hand dangled awfully and the wrist was sharp and angular and wrong. Sobbing, she looked away from the injury and reached down blindly with her good hand, fumbling with the knots around her ankles.

Finally free, she grabbed her arm again and stood, weeping as she staggered across the kitchen. The chair tumbled away behind her but the sound didn't register: thick, throbbing tendrils of pain strangled her arm and pumped icy cold blood back into her chest. Her whole body was numb.

"Henry…" she whispered, stumbling into the entrance hall. The whole house felt like it was shuddering and she moved on unsteady feet, crossing the tiles in a haze of agony until her body flopped into the front door. Screaming as she let go of her left hand and it fell painfully to her side, the bones smacking each other loosely, she grabbed the doorknob with her right and twisted it open.

The door fell inward and she tumbled outside, only stopping when she had careened onto the gravel at the bottom of the stone steps. The world swam and whirled around her.

"Henry!" she called, looking up into the cloud of red paste swilling in her vision. "Henry—"

Her eyes swept past the carriages in the driveway, past the lawn and the forested area at the edge of the grounds; she looked toward the front gates and balked.

The wrought-iron gates were under siege.

Darcy watched, horrified, as one of her father's guards thrust the serrated blade of a bayonet rifle into the gut of a great armoured bear-creature, twisting the weapon into its belly and throwing it off the gates. Behind him a second of the things was climbing, bone-white spikes rolling across its muscular body as it twisted its body up the brickwork beside the gate and reaching the top with ease. It looked back down at the guard and roared, its mouth opening in a great display of vicious teeth, eyes flaring brightly.

The guard screamed as thick claws plunged into his stomach and shredded it to viscous ribbons of red. Collapsing onto his knees, he was trampled by the first beast as it followed its armoured brother up the wall. A dozen feet away, a second guard was wrestling with something that looked like a clump of jelly with lashing tentacles; behind him, more of the things slipped through the bars of the gates.

They were getting out, Darcy realised. All these mad creations… they were going to get out. And once they were out there, there would be no stopping them.

Massacre.

She jolted at the sound of an angry hiss above her and looked up. In her periphery, the second guard screamed, the sound a harrowing whistle in the miasmic cloud of emotions she was experiencing.

An enormous, moss-covered stone snake crawled

over the manor house's roof toward her, its eyes blazing. Its mouth opened as it slithered forward, fangs the length of her arms bristling with hunger and spittle.

"Shit," Darcy murmured, backing up and staggering onto the doorstep. The forest exploded with noise and she saw ghostly figures flickering at the edges of the trees, their faces speckled with sunlight, eyes bright white points. One of the armoured beasts had slipped over the wall and the other was following. As she watched in awe, the second guard's head was twisted off his body with a winging expulsion of blood-red ichor and the jelly-creature attached to him sunk its tentacles into the mess of his throat, pulling out meat and muscle and tossing them in globs onto the gravel.

The snake above her lashed out. Darcy cried out as she ducked beneath its snapping jaws, a wave of hot air smacking her face. She turned and crashed through the front door, slamming it behind her.

Roman grabbed Henry by the shirt and slammed her into the wall, spittle flying into her face as he laughed.

"Didn't I tell you to stay out of the icehouse?" he seethed. "Didn't I fucking tell you? I gave you a headstart, Henrietta. You remember that? I let you into my fucking house – I didn't punish you for *snooping* – even though your name wasn't on my fucking list; remember *that*? Remember how *kind* I have been to you? And now you come down here, you… you arrogant little *snot*, and you try and tell me that what *I'm* doing is wrong?"

He let go and she slid down the wall, the back of her skull screaming with pain.

"I am a god," Roman whispered, pointing a trembling finger at her. His whole body shook with anger. "I am creator and destroyer; do you understand what I've done, bitch? What I've achieved? To harness the power of imagination and make its fancies real… the things I could do with that power. And you *dare* think you can stop me? This doesn't stop at exotic creatures, Henrietta. It doesn't stop at an *army* of creatures."

Henry groaned, grabbing the back of her head where it had smacked the stone wall behind her. Blood trickled through her fingers. The upstairs was rumbling above them, the vast chamber of the basement laboratory shuddering as though rocked by an earthquake. The machinery whirred and wheezed so loudly that Roman's voice was half-lost in the mess.

"I can do anything," Roman growled, crouching down to her level. "I can change the world, Henrietta. And I *will*. With this technology, I can—"

There was movement across the laboratory. Henry's eyes flitted toward the vague blur, just past Roman's shoulder. Frowning, he turned his head to look.

"Incredible," he whispered. Behind him Barron

twitched in his chair, the cables snaking from his exposed brain pumping surreal strings of energy into the walls. The author had twisted somehow in his seat, and now he was looking in their direction, his eyes rheumy and vacant but possessed by something they had not held before.

He was awake.

"Stay down," Roman said softly, twisting his fingers into Henry's hair and slamming her head into the wall again. Pain rushed into her brain and she moaned, disoriented, watching as he stood and moved to the author's chair. "What do we have here?" she heard him say, his voice travelling to her through tar.

Barron's head tipped back a little, a thin trickle of grey pulp running down his forehead. Upstairs the top of his skull had fallen to the floor, Roman's prized 'Moondisc' lying in a pool of shattered glass pieces.

"Good to see you again, Barron," Roman said quietly, his voice tainted with a smug, controlled electricity. "I didn't think you'd ever wake up again, you know. I am glad you got to see what we've achieved together."

Barron murmured something, his tongue lolling against his teeth, the words slurred and unintelligible. Henry grunted as she grabbed the workbench-top above her and heaved herself to her feet.

Roman was distracted, busy trying to figure out what Spencer Barron was saying. "Don't waste your energy, my friend. Keep that imagination focused. We wouldn't want any of your creations to become inattentive, now, would we?"

Barron's head rolled. He slurred something again, but his voice was useless.

"I must say, they've proven themselves quite autonomous," Roman mused, slipping his hands into his pockets. He grinned. "I don't think we'll need you at all, after a point. But I must thank you for providing the templates. And until I know your beasts can be… sustained, let's just keep you quiet, shall we? Hush, now. Hush…"

Henry leaned heavily on the workbench, looking up at the wall behind her. A small red spot marked the point on the stone where her skull had cracked open. Breathing heavily, she looked across the stonework and her gaze fell onto a bank of thick, glass tubes, arranged vertically. Viscous green glue bubbled inside each one. Shifting her weight, she curled her fingers around one of the tubes and held herself up with it.

Noticing her movement, Roman's eyes darkened and he stormed across the basement toward her. "You just keep dreaming, Barron," he called over his shoulder. "I'll be right back with you…"

He loomed over her, slapping her hand away from the glass tube. Henry wobbled, almost falling, but steadied herself on the bench.

"Leave that alone, bitch," Roman said. "I don't have

the patience for your fucking—"

"*Oo—wohn... geh—way...*" Barron slurred somewhere behind him.

Roman froze. Slowly, he turned his head.

"*Oowohn't... geh—way withiz...*"

"What?" Roman shook his head. "Speak up, old chap. You're not making any—"

"*You won't get away with this,*" Barron snarled, his eyes snapping up to meet Roman's.

Roman stared at him for a moment. Unseen, Henry reached up to wrap her fingers around the glass tube again. It was bracketed to the wall, sturdy enough to hold her up. She watched with a sick feeling in her stomach as Barron continued, drooling.

"All this…" Barron whispered. "I dreamed up all of this…"

Roman cocked an eyebrow. "Yes," he said. "Well done, you."

"The monsters," Barron slurred. "The… creatures."

"Quintessential elements of a good horror story," Roman said, smiling thinly. "Some of your best work."

Barron paused. His chest was heaving. He smiled back. "Something else…"

Henry swallowed. His eyes were rolling, and one of them had landed on her.

"Something… you've forgotten. Something every good story… needs," Barron murmured.

Roman laughed bitterly. "Oh, really? What's that?"

He was looking right at her now. And now Henry realised. Her stomach knotted up and her chest pounded as the revelation billowed through her. It didn't make sense. No, it couldn't be…

"I'm talking to you, Barron," Roman snapped. "What? What did I forget?"

Limply, with every ounce of energy he had, Spencer Barron smiled. "A protagonist."

Henry wrenched the glass pipe suddenly, propelling her entire body weight forward and yanking it from the wall. The ends of the tube shattered against the straining brackets and glass shards sprinkled the floor of the laboratory as a surge of bright green fluid splashed the workbench. Roman turned – too late – and Henry yelled with rage and fire as she gripped the shattered tube tightly, right in the middle, and rammed the jagged glass end directly up into his throat.

Roman gargled, clutching at his neck as the glass slid into his flesh and drew thick ropes of blood. He stared wide-eyed at Henry and she stared back, holding fast as she struggled, her face hard and emotionless.

"You…" Roman rasped, his body wriggling violently, blood pumping out of his neck and running in sheets down the inside of the glass tube, then pouring out onto the floor. It splashed her legs in droplets. Gritting her teeth, Henry twisted the pipe.

Roman slid to the floor and she let go, gasping and staggering back.

A tear ran down her cheek as she stared in Barron's direction. His head had fallen forward and he twitched awfully in his chair, alive still – she doubted the machines plugged into his body would ever let him die – but thankfully asleep.

Roman wheezed at Henry's feet, blood pooling from his neck, his movements becoming weaker and weaker. The glass tube fell from her hand and smashed loudly on the floor. She hardly noticed. Her parents… her life…

She couldn't remember any of it. And as she tried to, now, she felt that niggling again, right at the back of her throbbing skull. The voice telling her to stop trying, stop pushing… because there was nothing there to remember.

She wasn't real.

One of Barron's creations.

She had been all along.

Her chest heaved and she crashed into the bench behind her, tears streaming down her face. "Oh, God," she moaned, mania pulsing through her veins, "oh, God…"

Footsteps.

Henry wheeled around to see Darcy stumbling into the cellar, her eyes flitting from the girl to Roman and back again. "I had to," Henry whispered, clocking the hunting rifle in Darcy's arm. "I'm sorry, I had to—"

"I know," Darcy said. She held the rifle awkwardly and Darcy noticed that her left hand was hanging limp, bent at the wrist. Her hair was a mess, her face red. She looked in Barron's direction.

"Darcy," Henry said. "I'm… what are you doing?"

Darcy had lifted the rifle and it trembled in her arm, pointed squarely at Barron's face. "They're getting out," she whispered through tears. "The creatures… they're all getting out. I can't let that happen."

Henry sunk back against the wall, looked at Barron. "If you kill him," she whispered, "what happens to them?"

"The creatures?" Darcy's eyes flitted back to Henry. "They cease to exist. Everything going through those pipes"—she nodded to the ceiling—"stops flowing. Everything out there created by him – by this machine – *stops*."

Henry opened her mouth. "You can't, I…"

She trailed off. Her mouth closed again. Her chest was trembling, her body weak and crumpling. *Tell her*, she thought. *Just tell her. You can figure out another way to stop the creatures. Together. You can be together. Just…*

"Do it," she whispered, swallowing.

"We're going to be okay," Darcy said, laying her finger on the trigger. "We're getting out of here. If I do this, it's all over."

I know.

Henry tumbled forward suddenly and she lurched toward Darcy, staggering through the aching and the blood, almost tripping on Roman's twitching body. Behind her the machines whirred menacingly.

Darcy grabbed her awkwardly and for a moment they stood together, the rifle pressed between them. Henry shook her head. "Before you… before you do it…"

"There's no time," Darcy insisted.

"There's time for this," Henry said, and she gripped both sides of Darcy's head and kissed her, hard. Tears ran down her face and melted into Darcy's and for a long, beautiful second they were together, frantic breaths mixing in the bristling, electric air.

Then Henry stepped back, nodding.

"Do it." She smiled sadly. "Make it stop."

Darcy looked at her, eyes wide with surprise and excitement and terror.

"You have to make it stop."

"Okay," Darcy nodded, her voice thin.

Henry closed her eyes. For a moment she had hope – perhaps he had lied – or perhaps she was safe down here, somehow – or perhaps—

The laboratory boomed with a sudden, deafening *clap*, and Spencer Barron's exposed brains slopped against the wall.

TIME

AND

THE

BEAR

Spangles of sunlight dappled the water, shallow crests foaming in the swelling shadow of a long, narrow bridge high above. Long sheer cliffs thrust out of the muddy edges of the river; at either end of the bridge, a wide scar of reddish earth was ruined by an explosion of treeline, thick green pine and aspen trunks swaying softly in the breeze.

A shape emerged from the eastern bank of trees, chunks of stone crunching beneath rugged walking boots. As if surprised to have escaped the cloying dark of the forest, the shape stopped, looked out upon the bridge, and closed its eyes with an expression that looked like relief.

Anders had made it.

Fingers tucked into the tight straps of a bulky, thirty-kilogram backpack, he swayed for a moment and breathed deeply, the cool wind caressing the thick, striated mess of an orange beard that, over many days, had covered his jaws and neck. His hair was long and tangled, his shirt stained green and black with soil. Sweat pooled in his armpits and between his legs, trickling down his back.

Reaching up to run a hand through his hair, Anders opened his eyes and took a cautious step toward the bridge. It must have been a good thousand yards long, wooden slats knitted to a framework of rope and twine that bowed in the middle, a great thin hammock of planks and netting that jounced even before he'd laid a foot upon it.

Standing right at the end of the bridge, Anders looked down into the softly-churning waters below and smiled. The air was cool and pleasant, the light of the slowly-waning sun a miasma of beautiful gold and pink. He was nearly home; the thought alone of sinking into a thick, foam mattress was incredible.

Drawing in a deep breath, Anders finally stepped onto the bridge.

A gargantuan weight barrelled into his back, vice-like jaws clamping down around his skull and puncturing the bone and cartilage of his neck. There was no time to scream; before he could react at all his head was ripped from his body in a savage spray of red and pink and all he could see was a yellowed, serrated set of teeth – then nothing—

1

—and then he emerged from the trees.

After a second that seemed to last an eternity, Anders blinked. He was standing where he had been only moments before, looking out onto the bridge. A few steps back, perhaps. Frozen stiff, he tried to blink away a smattering of black needlepoints in his vision. Shook his head.

Slowly, he reached up to feel his neck.

Was he dreaming?

The flesh felt real against the pads of his fingers, the bone beneath solid and intact.

But he still felt the sensation of enormously powerful jaws closing around his throat, ripping major arteries in a gushing explosion of hot, wet pain, tearing his head from his body…

He hadn't drunk a drop of alcohol in days, had only partaken of small and disappointing rations of marijuana since leaving the trail. Not enough to hallucinate, and certainly not after a few hours. Perhaps it was lack of sleep, or food. Perhaps the sensation was just that: a sensation. Déjà vu, maybe.

Stepping up to the bridge, he looked down into the water and frowned. The water sparkled in exactly the same way it had seconds ago.

Slowly, he turned.

And the bear smashed out of the trees in a streak of brown and black, its face ripped open in the centre where a great bony maw of teeth and thick, black tongue yawed into an enraged cavern. Thick, gnarled claws punched into Anders' chest and he stumbled backward onto the bridge, barely landing on his back before the bear twisted its head and closed its enormous jaws around his neck. Anders screamed, a spray of thick hot blood exploding out of his mouth as his spinal column was twisted open.

Pain.

And then—

2

—and then he emerged from the trees.

Anders staggered forward, his entire body shuddering as an overwhelming cloak of terror swaddled him, tightening around his throat. Both hands went to his neck and he felt desperately for any bite-marks, anything at all, but there was nothing. He was standing a little way back from the bridge, right where he'd been before…

Panicking suddenly, Anders turned around, gazing back into the trees. "What the hell is going on?" he whispered. The treeline was still, the only sounds the frantic pounding of his heart and the tinny rattling of batteries in his digital wristwatch as he raised his hands to run them through his hair.

His eyes flitted left and right, scanning the trees for movement. Nothing. Nothing there at all. Why would there be? There was no bear.

There was no bear.

Anders laid a hand across his chest, drawing deep breaths to try and slow his heartbeat.

No bear.

He'd imagined it. A brief spell of exhaustion-induced hallucination, that was all. And it was over now.

This time he heard it before he saw it, his ears attuned to the silence so that the splintering *crunch* of wood immediately drew his attention to the shadow barrelling out of the trees. But even then, it was too late: before he could take a single step back, he was screaming into the bear's mouth as a hot, wet cavern of teeth and tongue punctured his skull and crushed it into the pulp of his brain.

3

And then he emerged from the trees.

Anders doubled over as bile punched up his throat, an acid bath pouring out of his mouth as a dirty red rattail and spilling onto his boots. His wet sputtering turned to an agonised howl and he screamed into the earth, hands clamped over his ears. A distant clump of trees shook as a murmuration of fluttering black shapes erupted from its boughs, shocked from their roost by the deafening outpouring of confusion.

Neck sore from some non-existent, phantom pain, Anders wheeled around to face the trees. His gaze immediately settled on the spot in the treeline from which the bear had come.

Two tiny points of white light, so insignificant it was no wonder he hadn't seen them before, stared back at him from the dark between the trees.

A flash of hungry teeth.

"What the fuck," Anders breathed, then a titanic clawed paw smashed into one of the trees and the bear launched itself forward, black lips peeling back, the tiny points of its eyes becoming yellow pools of rage as they caught the sunlight.

Anders' eyes widened as he realised he knew what was coming next. He staggered back and to the side, breaking free of the stunned shell that had encased him and taking a single step out of the reach of the bear's swinging, slack jaws—

With a sickening *crack* the vice of the bear's maw burrowed into his shoulder, immediately dislocating his left arm and punching his ribs into his back. Anders' eyes bulged and he screamed in agony. Somewhere at the back of his skull a subconscious, flaring red part of his mind was momentarily relieved that at least the bear hadn't ripped his head off his neck this time. Then the bear ripped a chunk out of his shoulder and roared, an enormous broad shape looming over him and bellowing hot spittle and meat into his face.

It clapped, punching its paws into his skull and puncturing his brain instantly.

Everything went black.

4

Anders stumbled out of the trees and kept stumbling, head swimming, thick bolts of pain like lightning across his shoulder and chest. Glancing quickly back into the trees, he staggered forward and lurched onto the bridge, suddenly aware that even if he couldn't stop the bear from coming he could at least run from it.

Surely it wouldn't follow him onto the bridge. It was an animal – a huge animal, but nonetheless one that was sure to be just a little reluctant of throwing itself onto a narrow funnel of wood and string – and it was these thoughts that propelled Anders forward, slamming his heel onto the bridge and instantly rolling his ankle.

"Fuu—uuuck!" he yelled, tumbling onto his front on the bridge. It swung madly as his weight crashed into the slats, and as he reached out to grab the nearest rope support it swayed and bent with the movement.

A colossal weight slammed into his back and he screamed as bony claws pierced his flank and shoulder.

"Fuuuuu—"

The bear swung its jaws down and ripped a chunk of meat from his neck, slopping meat hungrily down its throat and punching Anders' convulsing body into the wood.

9

Anders stepped breathlessly out of the trees and staggered forward, not risking a look back, keeping his eyes on the ground as he lunged onto the bridge and heaved his body into a run.

Phantom pains erupted all over his body – echoes, memories of teeth and claws and broken bones – as the bridge bowed beneath his thumping feet. The backpack swung heavily on his back, the clattering of steel pots muffled through layers of clothing and waterproof material. His vision was foggy and black. He kept his eyes on the edge of the bridge, a good kilometre-plus away – a thousand yards, now – nine-hundred-ninety-five—

He wasn't fast enough.

The bear ploughed into him and Anders yowled as sharp knives raked his back, spraying the wood with blood. Warmth gushed down his spine as he tumbled into the rope supports, his neck snapping immediately as his skull caught in the netting and twisted.

15

Anders crumpled, stumbling out of the woods and crashing into the reddish dirt, his knees buckling beneath him as his whole body exploded with fatigue. When he had finished vomiting he tipped his head back and screamed.

The sound was enough to shake enormous clots of birds from the trees. He yelled until his throat was coarse as sandpaper and his voice cracked and died in his mouth, and then he sobbed into his hands, his face stinging and hot, his lungs burning.

"Why," he moaned, his voice barely a whisper.

The answer came in the form of a low, rumbling bellow behind him.

Anders wept, and as he cradled his skull in his hands the bear lurched up and loomed over his body and struck, plunging its claws into his neck.

24

It felt like half an hour had passed. But the sun still hung exactly where it had been before the bear; the clouds, what thin wisps of them stained the ichor of the sky, had not moved either. Far below him the same swell of water gushed beneath the bridge.

He stood at the edge of the woods for a good thirty seconds, just watching the sky.

Was this all there was? All there was going to be?

Anders had a sudden thought. Raising his wristwatch, he fumbled with the controls for a moment, a tiny beep accompanying every jab of a button. Satisfied that the settings were correct, he started the timer and watched.

One second.

Two seconds.

Three—

The shadow of the bear thrust out of the woods behind him and before Anders could count to four, his body was ripped in half in a warm spurt of blood and gore. Moments after he had died, parts of him began to plop into the water far below.

Quicker this time.

The second he stepped out of the woods, Ander looked at his wristwatch. Set the timer with a trembling hand and watched the display as the seconds snicked past. *One. Two. Three.*

Twelve.

Twenty.

Thirty-five.

He drew in a breath and held it, suddenly acutely aware of the presence behind him in the trees. He could sense it breathing on the air, feel its eyes boring into the back of his skull.

Forty-two.

The tiny *crack* of a dead branch as the bear took its first step forward.

Fifty.

Anders lowered the watch and counted in his head.

Seconds passed. A few of them, at least.

Then the left side of his skull smashed into the right and teeth the size of his thumbs splintered his jawbone in two.

32

He had timed it a few times now and it seemed apparent that he had about a minute – somewhere between fifty-five and fifty-nine seconds, anyway –

from the moment he stepped out of the woods to the very second the bear crushed his skull in.

What could he do in a minute?

He could run. He had tried a few times to make it across the bridge, but he never got far enough.

Well, run faster.

He could jump. Would the bear follow him over the cliff and into the river? Could he *make* a jump like that? If something *other* than the bear killed him, would the circadian loop he'd found himself in continue? Or would he just… die?

And what had caused all this? Was it the bear?

Was it him, somehow?

Or something else?

"Think," he whispered. "What can you do in sixty seco—"

His eyes bulged out of his head as his brain was ripped from his nervous system.

40

So, running wasn't an option.

There was no way he could make it across the bridge. At his best calculation – and this was only approximate, for he could only use his own exhausted judgement to gauge the length of the bridge – the gap between the cliffs was about a thousand yards. Maybe a few more. Call it a thousand, to be safe.

He remembered that Usain Bolt had run something

like forty-five kilometres an hour at his highest, which amounted to around seven hundred and forty-five metres per minute. Mentally, he calculated that to be about eight hundred and ten yards. Eight-fifteen, maybe.

So, if he could run at Usain Bolt speed, he'd make it eighty per cent of the way across the bridge. Nearly the whole length.

But Anders wasn't Usain Bolt. And so far, he had only been able to make it about one-fifth of the distance.

So what? You don't have to make it across the bridge.

You just have to outrun—

—the bear ploughed into him.

45

Anders launched straight into a sprint, lurching for the bridge at what he considered to be breakneck pace, even if it wasn't Bolt-speed.

He made it a good three hundred yards before the bear caught up to him, closing the distance in four or five long, loping strides and knocking into his spine. The bridge swayed side-to-side as they tumbled over each other in a rampage of brown-black fur and shredded skin. He knew the bear's face well by know. He looked into its eyes in that last moment, a glaring, hungry yellow.

The colour of death.

80

Something different.

Anders glanced at the sun – still there, hanging right on the horizon where it had been all this time, though he felt he'd been doing this for a good hour now. Then he turned around and ran back into the trees.

Forget the bridge.

He burst through a hanging network of vines and tumbled downhill, boots punching into the soft earth as dead things crackled and shifted around him. Trees flashed past as he raced through the undergrowth, ignoring the scratching and clawing of thick knee-high thorns and branches.

He'd been running for what felt like an hour when he cursed himself for not trying this before. Of course. It was the fucking bridge, that was when the loop had started – he just had to get out of range of it before the end of his minute, *that* was how he escaped this nightmare – why had he never tried running back into the woods?

Anders tore to the right and ducked a low-hanging branch. This is it, he thought frantically, this is my escape. Keep running, don't look back, don't think about it.

He didn't have time to think about it.

His whole body smashed into the moss-covered

trunk of a thick aspen and he collapsed, tipping backward – straight into the arms of the titanic bear that had followed him from the treeline.

A minute had passed. Blood spattered his wristwatch.

123

How do you deal with a bear attack?

As far as Anders recalled, it was one of two things. Either you stood as tall as possible and tried to intimidate the bear – make as if to fight it, if necessary – or you cowered, showed submission, let it know *you* know who's in charge.

There was no third option.

There was no *run*.

He had been going about this entirely wrong. He had to turn round, look the bear dead in the eyes, face it head-on.

Anders turned. Looked in the direction of the watching bear. Decided upon option one, and stood as straight as he could muster. This had to be it.

And if not, you'll have the chance to try again.

The bear lumbered out of the woods.

Anders' body tightened and he growled, narrowing his eyes.

It was a grizzly. He had known this for some time now, though classifying the animal hadn't been high on his list of priorities. He remembered every time the

128

bear had slaughtered him, still felt every agonising, shredding pain; there wasn't an inch of his body that hadn't been torn or pulped or punctured.

Anger enveloped him suddenly and he roared, lunging toward the bear with his hands flexed into knotted, white-knuckled hooks. "Come on, then!" he yelled. "Come fucking fight me, if you think you're hard enough!"

Option one wasn't it.

The bear smashed its whole weight into him and Anders toppled onto his rucksack in the dirt, thick claws punching into his gut and ripping out coil after coil of intestine as he twitched and gargled.

124

Option two, then.

Anger still pumping through him, mania immediately filling his veins, Anders turned and slung off the backpack. It landed with a rattling *thwump* in the dust.

Eyes locked on the bear, Anders lowered his head in submission and dropped to his knees.

Be small. Don't let it think you want to fight.

Briefly he wondered if the grizzly could remember all of this, too. What if this mad, repeating minute wasn't localised to him? What if it was the whole world? Everybody had been living out the same minute for the past two hours, again and again, and they would forever… it was a glitch in the system, something had suddenly and fundamentally broken in the universe and time was ruined.

Or maybe it was just him and the bear. Locked together in this moment because… well, because someone up there hated them both. Maybe if he died enough times, whatever mad god was doing this would be satisfied and take time off pause.

No, that couldn't be it. Curling his head into his chest, he breathed slowly and listened to the bear's padding footsteps. It had to be survival. That was his only way out. Survive this minute, and his life would continue as it had meant to.

And this was how he survived. By treating the bear as a superior, by showing it he meant no harm. *This was*

125

Anders closed his eyes and stifled screams.

The bear came for him after fifty-nine seconds, as it always did.

He began again.

159

And began again.

180

246

Again.

500

Again.

2,789

Anders tumbled forward, scrambling for the cliff edge. He didn't care if plummeting into the river killed him for real. Ended him.

He just wanted this to stop.

He rolled over the edge and for a second he was flying, then that second seemed to stretch into an eternity, wind whistling past his ears, the long stripe of the bridge above him shrinking, growing narrower as his arms flailed uncontrollably and he rolled over himself, again, again, crashing down toward the water below—

His head smashed into the cliff edge and he bounced. Left foot jolted into his knee, bone shearing

131

flesh, as a boulder punched upward. Water surface smacked him hard.

He floated, stars swimming in his vision, blood pooling into the river around him and turning to thick clots of red mist. The water was unbelievably cold, immediately freezing his veins. He gazed up, into the sky, musing upon the permanence of death. That was how it should be.

Or maybe this was hell. Maybe he was doomed to repeat his last minute on Earth because whoever ruled this nightmarish afterlife had decided that was man's worst punishment.

He could have sworn a good eighty seconds had passed when the grizzly bear appeared at the cliff edge high above him, poking its face into his line of sight and growling down at the river.

Its ears twitched. And he saw something else, too: clinging to the bottom of the bridge, something small and worm-like and pale.

Then the grizzly leapt, ploughing off the cliff with all the grace and savagery of a bird of prey, and as it smashed into him and punched him underwater and he screamed with a mouthful of icy, wet silt and blood, he thought:

At least it was different this time.

5,012

Anders staggered out of the trees and fell onto his face,

where he lay in the dirt and waited for death.

He had tried everything he could think of. When these attempts had failed, hundreds of times each, he had tried them all again. And again. And again.

He went through periods of depression where he didn't bother at all, just crumpled in the sand and let it happen to him. Then, when even this grew tiring, he seemed to build up an urge to try again, to refuse defeat and try something else. Or, more accurately, something he had already tried more often than he could count. The bear couldn't be outrun, or fought – he had spent hours upon hours of repeated minutes digging items out of his backpack to use as a weapon, and each had been unsuccessful – and it couldn't be submitted to, dominated, tricked.

After he had tried a few more things, he fell into his depression again.

A cycle within a cycle.

Even when he drowned – smashed his face on a tree – stumbled into a wild dog's den in the woods – got bitten by a snake – the loop restarted. Didn't matter if the bear killed him, or the fall, or if – as he had begun to do, just lately – he found a way to kill himself.

It never ended.

Was it a lesson?

"Doesn't matter," he murmured into the dirt. "Bear's coming."

The padding footsteps loudened and he closed his eyes.

31,780

All his agony was mental.

His body reset, just like everything else, at the beginning of every minute. He was only as tired, as hungry, as thirsty as he had been at the start of it all.

But he hadn't eaten or drunk anything in what felt like a month, and he hadn't slept. His body was completely unwounded, but he had suffered every imaginable injury and death over and over, one after the other in an unrelenting, exhausting pattern.

Mentally, there was nothing left of him. Every time he emerged from the treeline he was weaker, lesser, closer and closer to real, permanent death. But it was like approaching an asymptote: it didn't matter how he *felt*, because physically, he was fine.

Until the bear came.

Again, just like before, it did.

90,505

This time he walked right into its arms, almost begging it through tears to just get it over with, kill him already.

It seemed to relish the kill more this time, playing with him, ripping softly, tearing chunks from his face and stomach with its teeth, almost nuzzling him.

It did this for about a minute, then it severed his carotid and he flopped limply into its mouth.

420,686

A fever dream.

He woke, hot and dazed, and the bear was above him, but further away than before. Then he was sinking into the Tartarus of its mouth, sinking, sinking…

Flies buzzed around the open door of the cabana and the ocean outside swelled softly. Food poisoning. The shrimp. He threw up again.

Claws plunged into his stomach and his cheek grazed the dirt.

851,000

Anders remembered something. Something he had seen… months ago? Weeks? Days?

About a minute ago, he supposed.

Something pale and worm-like, suckered to the bottom of the bridge.

"Huh," he said, stumbling forward a step. Maybe he should look for—

1,904,371

Anders lunged forward, shucking the backpack from his shoulders and scrambling onto the bridge. The nineteenth plank, he remembered. That was the weakest. Thundering forward, he counted – *three, eight, fourteen—*

Nineteen.

Dropping to his knees, he fumbled desperately with the plank. He had done this so many times now that he knew just how to pull, just how to lever the wretched thing so that it ripped loose from the bracing rope on the left within a few seconds. Then all he had to do was catch the damn thing before it—

The slat tore away in his hands, exposing a sliver of nothing in the bridge through which he saw the river below.

Something pinkish and gelatinous slithered away from him, a wet sucking sound accompanying the slug-like movement of the thing beneath the bridge.

"Fuck you!" Anders yelled, thrusting his arm through the gap and fumbling about beneath the bridge. He slapped something warm and wet, felt it squirm as he grabbed frantically for it. His fingers clutched it and he heaved back, cringing at the putrid smell and the feeling of warm, meaty slime in his hand. "Come here, you bastard!"

Claws in his back. His grip loosened and he fell forward, succumbing instantly to the jaws that clamped over his neck and ripped his head off his body.

2,000,192

Lunge forward. Lose the backpack.

Bridge. Nineteenth plank. He'd tried the rest; not

loose enough. Or too far away.

Drop. Grab. Wrestle—

The plank came loose and he jammed both arms down through the hole. Grabbed, swiping at thin air until—

Practically hugging the thing, he heaved with all his strength and squeezed its wriggling, hissing body up between the slats and onto the bridge.

It lashed out with a stubby, segmented tail, its piercing cry one of irritation, not pain. And then it writhed out of his hands, slopping onto the bridge in a blur of pink and white and rolled away, plummeting off the side of the bridge and toward the water, leaving him empty-handed.

"NO!" he screamed, scrambling to the edge of the bridge. "NOT AGAIN! PLEASE!"

The bear came.

2,304,332

Forward. Backpack. Bridge.

Nineteen.

Pull. Grab.

Lumbering footsteps behind him as he slammed the worm-thing's wriggling body onto the bridge and pinned it.

"What the fuck is going on?!" he yelled into its face. It squirmed, its face nothing more than a ring of teeth in a shallow black pit. It squawked as he slammed his knee into its segmented midsection. It was the size of a pillow, a little longer maybe, with barbs and bumps beneath its membrane-coated skin. "Tell me! What the fuck is—"

Bear.

2,558,701

Nineteen.

Grab.

"What's happening to me?" Anders screamed, slamming the worm into the wooden slats of the bridge.

It hissed, its round maw yawing open, hooked barbs shooting out from within like thin, black tongues.

"ANSWER ME!"

Bear.

4,068,942

"Answer!" Anders yelled, launching his fist into the worm-thing's face. Barbs sunk into his skin; he ignored them. "Tell me why you're doing this!"

The worm screeched. Anders shook it, begging through tears.

"Answer me, answer me! Please, just fucking answer me, please!"

Bear.

19,540,328

*"PLEASE, FOR THE FUCKING LOVE OF GOD,
ANSWER ME!"*
Bear.

384,701,888

Bear.

700,382,901

"Please—"

"Fine!" the worm shrieked, its voice strangled and
unnatural. "Fine, just… just stop! Jesus!"

Stunned, Anders's grip loosened and he recoiled.
Blinked.

It wasn't real. Couldn't be. He was hallucinating.

He'd finally – after ten, fifteen, twenty, *however
many* years of this – gone completely, irrecoverably
mad.

"Make it stop," he whispered.

"*Fine,*" the mucus-covered creature hissed.

When Anders looked over his shoulder, there was
no bear.

Then, to his horror, it lumbered out of the trees. An
enormous, shadowy shape, its face locked in a tight,
knotted mask of hunger and unadulterated predatory

rage. Its claws hung by its sides, huge and glinting in the fading sunlight.

It stood at the end of the bridge and watched him.

"What the hell is this?" Anders breathed. "Why isn't it coming?"

Before the worm-creature could answer, the bear exploded.

Anders screamed as the grizzly detonated into a visceral slop of blood and bone, furry hunks of flesh spattering the bridge as more rained into the river and streaked the cliff with red. "What the fuck?!"

He turned back to the worm.

"What are you? Start fucking talking, now!"

The worm spoke, and its voice was like the shrieking of a faraway baby. Its whole body rippled and wobbled as its jaws moved. "I am time," it said.

"What the fuck does that mean?"

"I have been here for a long time," it whispered. "I *am* time. Do you know the things I can do?"

"I've been fermenting a few theories," Anders said gruffly. "Why are you doing this to me?"

For a second that seemed to last a lifetime, the worm looked up at him with its awful, eyeless face. Finally, it giggled. "I've been... playing."

Anders fumed.

"I used to be like you, you know. Then I discovered myself. I can't die. Can't age. But as time moved around me – backwards, forwards, round and round in circles – I changed. Became... god. God of time. Time itself. Do you know what happens to a creature who lives for millions of eternities, caught in time, straddled by it… broken by it? A creature who has seen time move in every conceivable direction and been unchanged by it, even as its mind attunes to the endless?

"I.

"*Am.*

"Time."

Anders shook his head. "And what do you want with me?"

The worm grinned, hook-like teeth shivering in its gummy, circular mouth. "Just a few more minutes."

"No," Anders started, his eyes going wide. "No, you can't—"

A shadow fell over him and he looked up.

The bear roared and a hot, wet darkness swallowed him.

1,945,382,304

Anders was dizzy. Ever-dying. Never-dying. He sobbed endlessly, screamed into the mouth of the beast that chased him onto the bridge, again and again and againandagainandagainagainagain…

Time stretched and snapped around him. He had spent lifetimes in this minute, dozens of lifetimes. He was unchanged. And yet…

Bear.

The bridge was a sloppy, feverish blur in the landscape. The bear was coming. Time was endless. He was endless.

When he looked down, vision fading, madness seeping through his brain, he could swear that his arms had begun to shrink.

936,473,201,495,382,493,001

Time could contain him no longer. He could feel the worm's control of this endless relentless universe fading, feel his body slipping between moments, his features less defined, his limbs conjoining as cell growth and repair – all bodily functions – stopped, ceased, shut down by his irreparably declining mental state but forced into shape by his body, emerging from the trees again and again, each time smashed into a different configuration by the bear—

He had stopped feeling it. A long time ago, longer than he knew, he had stopped feeling pain.

Feeling anything.

He had forgotten his name. But that was *millennia* ago.

***

<u>ALSO AVAILABLE FROM THE AUTHOR</u>

Day of the Mummy
Night of the Bunny
Dark Nights (Stories)
Dead Engines (Horror Stories of the Railway)
Empire of Cold
Endless Living Organ Massacre
Drop Bear (Outback Terror: Book One)
Parliament of Witches
Burrow

9 781915 272850